DOCTOR'S

Although Dr Tessa Lane had only met Dr Giles Rutherford once, three years ago, the meeting had been a memorable—and passionate—one. Now, totally unexpectedly, he had come back into her life—and it looked as if this time he was going to stay . . .

Sonia Deane is a widow with one son, lives in the Cotswolds, and has written over 120 books. The Doctor-Nurse stories were fortuitous. She chose a doctor hero and from then her readers wanted a medical background. Having personal friends who are doctors enables Sonia Deane's research to be verified. She has also been out with an ambulance team and donned a white coat in hospital!

To Tony and Diana –
my son and daughter-in-law.
They will know why.

DOCTOR'S FORBIDDEN LOVE

BY

SONIA DEANE

MILLS & BOON LIMITED
15–16 BROOK'S MEWS
LONDON W1A 1DR

First published in Great Britain 1985
by Mills & Boon Limited

ISBN 0 263 75292 5

Set in 10 on 12 pt Linotron Times
03–0186–51,800

Photoset by Rowland Phototypesetting Limited
Bury St Edmunds, Suffolk
Made and printed in Great Britain by
Richard Clay (The Chaucer Press) Limited
Bungay, Suffolk

CHAPTER ONE

THEIR eyes met as he came into the crowded room, the gaze holding in surprised awareness while the memory of his long passionate kiss rushed back, and Tessa heard the echo of his voice saying, 'We shall meet again: this is not the end.' Emotion stirred as his magnetism made her realise that he had a power and fascination which she had never forgotten. Dr Giles Rutherford—a striking man in his early thirties, with strong features and a faint suggestion of the artistic to counteract any hardness. His mouth was firm, and she recalled that his smile had been a compelling mixture of gentle indulgence and genuine humour. She noticed, even in that second, how his dark hair swept back from a fine forehead and was attractively shaped. His grey eyes were direct and mesmeric.

In turn, he studied her. Tessa Lane, a doctor. Intriguing; with high cheekbones and deep blue eyes that shaded to violet—tantalising, provocative and yet tranquil in moments of calm. He liked her nut-brown hair, gold-flecked and shining, and the way she wore it curved loosely against her face. He even remembered the seductive habit she had of threading her fingers through it and then letting it fall naturally back into place. She was slim without any suggestion of bony thinness, and her small waist emphasised the firm rounded curves of her breasts.

Tessa watched him striding through the guests as though he had a right of way. When he reached her she said in a breath, 'What are you doing here?' Her directness was disarming and betrayed her nervousness. Their gaze still held.

'I came with Paul Mason—Dr Mason,' he explained. 'What are you doing here?'

She uttered Paul's name in faintly alarmed astonishment.

'You obviously know him.' There was a hint of interrogation in Giles' remark. But they realised that the conversation was not important, and that only the memories and their sexual attraction were real.

'I know him very well.' She didn't add that Paul wanted to marry her and was awaiting her decision. 'As to what I'm doing here,' her laughter was light, 'this is my parents' party and their house. My father has his practice here and I work with him. Didn't the name Lane mean anything to you? Paul must have mentioned it.'

His reply reached her with shock. 'It doesn't really matter how I got here—does it?' As he spoke his gaze deepened with an electrifying intimacy. 'Actually, Paul didn't mention names.'

Conscious of danger, she persisted, 'But what are you doing in Tewkesbury?'

He hesitated, then said a trifle evasively, 'Catching up with friends. I arrived from Singapore last evening and am staying at the Bell. Paul had no idea of my visit and when I telephoned him about our getting together, he warned me that, whatever happened, he was going to drag me off to a party this evening.' He added tensely, his voice low, 'I told you we should meet again.'

'That was three years ago.'

'So you remember?'

Emotion was like a pulse throbbing between them and she felt that he must hear her heart thumping.

At that moment Paul joined them, slightly breathless, having been called to the telephone which was switched over from his surgery to the Lanes' house, River Bank.

'Ah,' he said, smiling at Giles, 'so you've made yourself known . . . sorry about rushing off like that.'

Tessa began, 'We—'

But Paul hurried on, still addressing Giles, 'Have you met Adrian and Letty—Tessa's parents?' There was warmth and enthusiasm in his voice.

Giles and Tessa exchanged faintly apprehensive and bewildered glances. Paul had obviously assumed that their meeting had only just taken place, and while Tessa had intended explaining, Paul's acceptance and interruption had forestalled her. In a glance she and Giles tacitly agreed on silence.

Paul was an attractive thirty-two. He had a sympathetic personality and air of good humour, and ran his practice (also in Tewkesbury) alone, with the aid of a qualified nurse and secretary. He was overworked and had reached a stage where he accepted the fact that he needed a partner. Until now he had viewed the possibility with dismay, but, in a flash, the thought raced through his mind that if he could persuade Giles to join him, the set-up would be perfect. It was also, he thought, most likely a pipe-dream, since he had no idea of Giles' professional commitments, or even if he was based in England. Theirs had been a friendship cemented in student days, their subsequent meetings as sporadic and unheralded as now. Nevertheless a deep bond of friendship remained, and they always met as though the intervening years had not in any way endangered the continuity. Just then Paul couldn't recall having mentioned Giles to Tessa, at whom he glanced with an appreciation of her beauty as she stood there in her simple white dress which exposed enough of her figure to be artistic and seductive. She had obviously made Giles welcome and could be relied upon to rise to any occasion. All he himself wanted was for her to agree to marry him. He felt that he must have loved her even in an earlier life, so deep was his devotion, and he argued that if it were possible for Giles to join him his own workload would be halved, and he and Tessa could begin their married life in ideal circumstances. All these hopes flashed through his mind as he stood there, while he managed to say in a normal pleasant voice, 'Well, Giles, not sorry you came?'

Giles avoided looking at Tessa.

'As someone who isn't keen on parties,' he admitted frankly, 'I'm delighted you "dragged" me here.' He looked around him. 'All this is most attractive. I love these half-timbered Tudor houses and I love Tewkesbury, too, to say nothing of Gloucestershire being a beautiful county.' He paused imperceptibly before adding, 'I've always thought that I'd like to live in this part of the world.' He glanced at Tessa and swiftly lowered his gaze before adding, 'Coming back to it, I'm even more inclined to the idea.'

Tessa raised her gaze half-questioningly to his and then looked down at her slightly trembling hands. The sound of voices came in a wave and she wanted to escape, feeling suddenly afraid as though the peace of the June day had been threatened.

Paul's expression changed to delight and hope as he exclaimed, 'Then why don't you come here and join me in the practice? God knows I need help, and it would be ideal.'

There was a sudden dramatic silence. Giles looked stunned, and astonishment betrayed itself in his voice as he said, half-disbelievingly, 'I might take you up on that.'

Tessa, lips parted, flashed a startled glance to meet Giles' unnerving gaze, and for one dangerous moment she was lost to her surroundings, until she heard her father's voice saying, 'I've done all the circulating I can for the moment.' He smiled at Giles, and Paul immediately made the introductions.

Adrian Lane exclaimed, 'Do you three realise that you haven't even a drink? What kind of a party *is* this?'

Tessa hastened, 'I've only just had a moment with Giles—' She stopped. She was explaining, and adding to her own confusion.

Adrian made a sign to a waiter carrying a drinks tray, and within seconds they each had a glass of champagne.

Paul shot an anxious glance at Tessa and murmured so that only she could hear, 'All right?'

'Noisy,' she whispered back.

Adrian was talking to Giles. 'Singapore,' he said with interest. 'But you can't practise there.' It was a statement rather than a question.

'Oh no,' Giles replied. 'But my father had a practice there. I've been over to see him; he had rather a bad coronary.'

Adrian said quietly, 'I'm sorry,' and Giles knew that he meant it.

Adrian Lane was a man in his late fifties, greying at the temples, and with finely-drawn, sensitive features and an air of dignity which escaped any coldness. His hair and complexion were fair, and he had a healthy glow that went with fitness and a love of life. He and Tessa were very close, even if they clashed on a good many modern methods, but she knew he had a wisdom not to be found in any textbooks.

'Where's Letty?' asked Tessa, referring to her mother and gazing around her at the well-filled room.

'Caught by the town gossip,' chuckled Adrian. 'She's been trying to get away for goodness knows how long . . . ah! She's made it.'

Letty, ten years Adrian's junior, squeezed through the crush and beamed at them.

'My feet are killing me!' she gasped . . . 'Oh,' she added with an endearing smile as she noticed Giles, 'I don't know you, do I? I'm Letty, Tessa's mother, and I hope you know Tessa, or I'm sunk.' She leaned against Adrian. 'Support me,' she added laughingly.

Tessa heard the remarks, smiled, but nothing registered. She was conscious of Giles' presence to the exclusion of everything else and couldn't think beyond him. It was like being taken out of her comfortable cocoon and tossed into an emotional maelstrom. Memories of their first, and only, meeting flooded back. It was at a spur-of-the-moment party, given by a couple they hardly knew, and to which each had gone without enthusiasm. Their mutual attraction had been instant, Giles remaining at her side whenever possible during the evening. At that time she was living in London and working at St Mark's Hospital where she had trained, without any thought of joining her father. Giles was in partnership with his brother, but was leaving for Singapore the following day to visit his parents who lived there. In retrospect, she bitterly regretted that their exchange of personal details had been so sketchy, and that she had not invited him in to her Kensington flat when he had driven her home in the early hours of that June night. Fear lest she might not have the courage ultimately to send him away, and reluctance to plunge into a precipitate affair with a stranger, prompted the caution. Nevertheless his long passionate kiss, and the words that had accompanied it in parting, had remained in her memory like jewels in a safe. She had not been naïve enough to give the interlude stability. Everyone flirted at parties, and for a few minutes borrowed the magic from love. Now there were so many questions she wanted to ask; so many gaps to be filled in, and she wondered, rather bleakly, if this occasion would be a question of history repeating itself. Yet he had *remembered*. Again, she argued, that there was always one special encounter that lingered enchantingly from the past. Reality might break the spell.

Letty, still youthful, with soft brown eyes and thick lustrous hair, was both witty and attractive—and very perceptive. She smiled at Tessa and asked drily, 'Will you be joining us some time?' Then, aware of the tense and somewhat distracted expression on Tessa's face, she added swiftly, 'The noise on these occasions—'

'If you will have birthdays,' Adrian teased.

'Sh-h-h! Only our close friends know that—not the patients.'

Giles immediately wished her many happy returns and admonished Paul for not letting him into the secret.

Letty wondered if Giles lived in the district and, if so, why hadn't she met, or heard, of him. He was far too attractive a man to pass unnoticed.

In that moment Tessa exclaimed with professional urgency, '*Karen!*'

Karen Meredith, family friend and Tessa's patient, flaxen-haired, twenty-four, sat upright, gripping the arms of a Regency chair on the opposite side of the room, her face a greyish-blue as she fought for breath in an asthmatic spasm. Guests stood nearby, helpless and panic-stricken.

The word oxygen flashed between Tessa and her father, who hurried in the direction of his consulting room, while Tessa—Giles and Paul following her—reached Karen's side, dispersing the onlookers. Without hesitation the two men lifted the suffocating figure, keeping her in an upright position, and, bandy-chair fashion, took her swiftly to join Adrian who had the oxygen cylinder ready, and applied the mask even as Karen was lowered on to a chair.

Tessa shook her head as they waited for the attack to subside. 'She must have forgotten her inhaler.'

In a few minutes the drama was over, and Karen breathed without help. Her chest was tight, her heart-beats slowing down with her pulse rate, as she murmured, her voice having the huskiness of an asthmatic, 'I'm so *sorry*. I changed handbags and left my inhaler behind . . . someone started smoking and was wearing heavy scent.'

'Let's get you out into the air,' Tessa said quietly.

'I'm upsetting everything.' Karen looked enquiringly at Giles.

Tessa made the introduction as they walked slowly from the consulting room—a spacious, well-equipped room, with white walls and red-and-white Regency striped curtains—into a secluded part of the garden, where Karen sat down on a cushioned hammock. She didn't feel like facing up to the rest of the evening, and a wave of depression washed over her as she realised anew the hazards of a condition with which she had lived since childhood.

Tessa, assessing Karen's nervous tension, while appreciating that anxiety, stress or upheaval triggered off asthmatic attacks, asked gently, 'Would you like me to run you home? I know your car is in dock and that you came with the Abbots . . .'

There was relief in Karen's half-apologetic, 'I feel such a *nuisance* . . .'

'Nonsense,' Adrian said heartily. 'We'll make up for it when your parents get back from Canada.'

'I miss them,' Karen said involuntarily, and, watching her, Tessa was aware of the underlying strain. She was a highly-strung girl who relied on the support of her family, having a brother and sister who ran an antique shop in Broadway.

Giles said somewhat surprisingly, 'We could come with you.' He glanced at Paul.

Paul said easily, 'Ah! A good idea, but I've to dash off to give an injection—you go.'

Tessa, excited, unable to fight against the emotion suddenly surging over her, gave a little laugh. 'I *am* capable of driving the three miles to Bredon!'

Karen urged, 'I should feel happier if you had someone with you. It wouldn't seem that you'd been dragged away from the party—I hate the thought of being a wet blanket.'

Tessa put a hand on her arm and smiled as she said, 'It's settled.'

'I'll explain to the Abbots,' promised Adrian, '*and* say goodbye to Letty. No need for you to go back into that stuffy atmosphere.' He kissed her and hurried away.

Paul got into his car as Tessa and the others drove away.

Tewkesbury—site of the final battle of the Wars of the Roses, and dominated by the magnificent Abbey, with its massive Norman tower—lay deserted in the evening light, its ancient Church Street and High Street, linked by the Memorial Cross, whispered of the past; the half-timbered, black-and-white buildings, lanes and courts, bearing testimony to the history of medieval days. The silence and peace was emphasised by the presence of the Rivers Avon and Severn flowing nearby.

'A place to explore,' said Giles with appreciation as they reached the end of the High Street, passing the Tudor House Hotel where Charles II was said to have hidden in the attic after the Battle of Worcester, and which was the Court of Justice during James I's reign.

'All the houses and hotels have a story to tell,' Tessa commented as she followed the Bredon sign ahead, leaving the river and the Worcestershire road to her left. The village was north-east of Tewkesbury, on the Avon, its fourteenth-century church spire visible for miles, while Bredon Hill rose impressively in the near distance, its wooded slopes etched against a cloudless blue sky, and encircling the 'Hill Villages of Bredon', famous for their picturesque beauty.

The car seemed to be filled with some powerful force which Tessa found overwhelming. She was conscious only of Giles sitting in the back, his presence like a magnet drawing her irresistibly to him.

His deep voice trailed away as he said, 'I didn't realise how beautiful all this is. The hawthorn hedges—'

'At their best last month,' said Karen, 'just a wall of snow.'

Tessa, after a short while, turned left at a cutting known locally as 'By the Seat'—the bus stop—and so into Church Street, almost facing Drapers— a splendid village store-cum-mini supermarket, delicatessen, bakery and Post Office, built up by the Draper family over the years—and then down past half-timbered houses and the black-and-white thatched Fox and Hounds inn and restaurant, where the cuisine compared favourably with its London contemporaries.

The Meredith house, Avon View, was near the church and river, and when Tessa stopped outside it she said to Karen, 'I just want a word with you.'

Karen looked, and felt, forlorn and lonely, wishing she had not left the party, her moods dictated by her immediate physical condition. She looked up at Giles as he opened the car door for her. 'Thank you for helping with the bandy-chair.'

Tessa went into the house with professional purposefulness. Mrs Yates, an old family retainer who had almost been a nanny to Karen over the years, came forward into the hall, alarm on her thin pale face.

'It's all right, Mrs Yates,' Tessa said reassuringly, 'the heat, smoke, and scent were too much.' Karen, she knew, would fill in the details.

Mrs Yates shook her head. Miss Karen (she refused to indulge in the modern trend for Christian names and familiarity which offended her old-fashioned susceptibilities) was far better away from crowds of people. But you couldn't tell the young, she thought regretfully, asthma or no asthma.

'Please don't worry about me,' said Karen, as Tessa went into the sitting-room, after Mrs Yates had left them.

'I *won't* any more than is necessary,' Tessa said firmly, 'provided I can feel sure you won't go out again without your inhalers. You know how vital they are . . . and I want to give you a check-up . . . don't argue—' her voice was protective despite the correction. 'Make an appointment with Mrs Wallace (the practice secretary) and come to the surgery. Now let me see—' Tessa was mentally recapping to make sure her instructions were being carried out, 'you're having two puffs of Ventolin and two of Becotide four times a day, including night and morning. And you rest for twenty minutes in the morning before you get up?'

'Yes. I couldn't cope otherwise . . . then there's the large doses of cortisone! I get weary of it all,' Karen added.

'Better that than being in hospital,' Tessa said gently, thinking of the many times Karen had been rushed there in the middle of the night when she'd caught any infection.

'Oh, I *know* . . . and you've been so good to me.' It was an apologetic, almost humble, sound. 'And now you get back to that devastating man! I envy you. God help his patients—they must all be in love with him!'

Giles watched Tessa come out of the house. She looked beautiful in the evening sunlight which sprayed her hair with a golden sheen, and emphasised her smooth tan. Her eyes met his, but they didn't speak as he opened the driving seat door and then, when she was settled, got into the car beside her.

Words burst out involuntarily, 'Would you like to have a look at my cottage?'

'Very much.' He sounded pleasurably surprised.

She drove towards Kemerton, turning off down a concealed lane which gave absolute privacy, and brought them to Chestnut Cottage, which took its name from a magnificent tree that stood in the small, old-fashioned walled-in garden.

'This was converted from stables,' she explained a few minutes later. 'I didn't want to live at home when I joined my father in the practice two years ago, despite getting on so well with my parents. I have a consulting room here where I can see any overflow of patients, or those who live in the immediate area.'

'It's delightful,' said Giles, standing beside her so that his nearness was like a magnet.

The cottage was a one-storey building, long and low, its roof gabled and built of Cotswold stone which gleamed golden as the sun struck it. Clematis trailed over the front door, and jasmine clung to one wall, its scent filling the air with a sensuous fragrance.

Tessa's hands trembled slightly as she opened the front door and they went inside. The original beams were exposed in high ceilings which gave it character that was reflected in a large sitting room, dining area and two bedrooms, with bathrooms en-suite, plus the consulting room. A pinky-mushroom carpet was fitted throughout the house, allowing for contrasting colours of gold and pale jade to harmonise. Giles walked through the rooms with obvious appreciation. They reached the bedroom—feminine, with lilac furnishings and built-in white furniture, the dressing-table decorative, with wing mirrors.

'I wanted to get away from "ye olde worlde",' she explained.

He looked down at her—a look that deepened to passion.

'Into a world of contradiction,' he said, his voice low and compelling.

She moved to the door, his nearness disturbing. It seemed like a fantasy to be here with this man whose kiss had enthralled her, its memory lingering over the years, making every other flirtation empty by comparison.

'Life *is* a contradiction,' she flashed at him, and led the way to her consulting room.

'I never know whether we choose our own pattern for living, or fate decrees it for us,' he said, and there was an uneasiness in the utterance.

Tessa's eyes opened wide in an unspoken question. It was as though he was trying to tell her something, and didn't quite know how.

'And you don't miss hospital life?' he added.

'Do *you*?' She wanted him to fill in the gap; to explain away the lost years; and she wanted to be in his arms —wanted it with an aching desperation that she had never experienced before.

He lowered his gaze guardedly. 'I've a great deal to sort out,' he said.

Paul's offer lay between them—to her, tantalisingly. Giles' words, 'I may take you up on that', offered hope.

They walked to the door together, so close that she could feel his oatmeal-shaded jacket brushing against her arm, and the faint warmth of his body.

He met her gaze with a deep penetrating intensity as attraction flared and he moved nearer, about to lower his lips to hers, when suddenly, as though some invisible hand had drawn him back, he turned away and said abruptly, 'Have dinner with me next week.'

Tessa was confused, her heart pounding.

'Very well,' she agreed shakenly, wondering why he hadn't kissed her.

'I'll ring you. What's your number?'

She gave it to him and he wrote it in his diary.

Tessa never forgot that moment, with the sun's rays slanting through the window, falling on the desk calendar as though prophetic. The bright airy room seemed to be waiting for some dramatic happening, and every piece of furniture was no longer merely an inanimate object, but a link between them; a bond in their medical life. The faint smell of ether hung in the air and suddenly, reluctantly, brought her back to reality.

'We must go,' she said.

'Yes.' Giles' sigh was deep. 'Thank you for bringing me here. It's right for you.'

As they left the cottage everything was still. Beyond the garden, fragrant with old-fashioned flowers, the distant fields shimmered in the golden haze of ripening barley. To their right, Bredon Hill rose majestically, while immediately ahead the Malverns were outlined against the sky like a vast frieze above the wooded landscape. Tessa felt that her world was suddenly illuminated. It wasn't what Giles had said, but what he had conveyed, that made it seem that they were two lovers who had reached the heights of ecstasy in those last seconds.

They drove back almost in silence through the quiet historic town, past the Bell Hotel which, allowing for reconstruction, bore the date 1696. Within a few minutes they reached River Bank with its views of the Avon and the cathedral.

Giles flashed Tessa an intimate glance when the car stopped, and swiftly reached her door, taking her hand, his fingers tightening on hers as he helped her to her feet, his touch electrifying.

A voice said, 'Hi, good timing!' Paul spoke as he drew up and braked beside them.

Tessa felt that she had been on a long journey and could not adjust to normal surroundings. But she managed to say, 'I showed Giles my cottage.'

'A delightful place,' Giles put in.

Paul looked pleased. He wanted Tessa to like Giles, and he wanted him for a partner.

'You should have seen the photographs before they started the conversion!' he grinned. 'It isn't every day you can have cocktails where the horses used to be fed!'

'True,' Giles murmured. He didn't look at Tessa, but

they were aware of each other as though tied by some invisible bond. *'I'll ring you.'* Those words became the most important of the evening. Tessa longed to be alone for a few moments to adjust to events and her own emotional turmoil, but departing guests milled around her and she was thankful it had only been a drinks party and not one where a buffet would have dragged it out until all hours.

'You'll stay on,' Paul said to Giles. 'The Bell's only a stone's throw away.' Paul spoke as though he himself was a member of the household.

'I'd like to,' came the firm reply, and for a second Giles glanced at Tessa, whose gaze lost itself in his.

'Must have a word with Tom Wright over there,' said Paul suddenly. 'Won't be a second.' He shot off across the room.

'Tom's a mutual friend,' Tessa explained. 'Anaesthetist . . . We like to have him on our cases.'

But Giles wasn't listening as he said quietly, 'You look just as I've remembered you.' The words were almost a solemn declaration.

Her lips parted as a tremor went over her. They were still standing in the hall, now deserted, oblivious of time and place, as tension mounted and desire touched the edge of pain.

'Tessa—' he began urgently, 'there's something—'

At that moment a pale-faced woman of about thirty appeared tentatively at the open front door.

'I'm so sorry to come uninvited, but—' she seemed to be swaying as she spoke, 'but I'm Rosemary Wynn, Dr Rutherford's fiancée,' she added, before she saw Giles come into focus through the blinding evening sunlight.

Giles paled and groaned inwardly, and even in that moment of drama asked himself: How did a man tell a woman he could not marry her, and had known it before he left for Singapore? And that was why he had avoided a reunion that day—playing for time?

Tessa froze; her skin seemed to lift from her flesh, the shock absolute.

But before anything could be said, Rosemary Wynn gasped, 'Giles! So . . . sorry . . .' And with that she slumped to the floor.

Professionalism took over as Tessa saw the red stain seeping around the inert figure's grey-and-white silk dress. Giles knelt quickly down beside her.

'Bring her into my consulting room,' ordered Tessa, thankful there were no onlookers.

Giles lifted Rosemary in his arms and followed Tessa. Once the patient was on the examining couch, Tessa exclaimed with quiet, icy authority, 'Leave us. And explain to the others,' she added witheringly.

Giles hesitated, but aware that Rosemary was coming round and that Tessa was already bending over her, taking her pulse, he went painfully and silently away, mindful that Tessa was a doctor and that he was a guest in the house.

Tessa became only the doctor in those minutes. She wanted facts—medical facts; personalities could not be involved. Nevertheless her trained eye saw Rosemary as a pretty woman with fair complexion and gentle blue eyes which now focused her with dismay. Her brown hair was naturally curly and fell loosely about her head in a style unsophisticated but attractive. Fear, anxiety and embarrassment brought confusion as she whispered, 'Where's Giles?'

'I sent him away. I'm Tessa Lane—a doctor—in practice here with my father. Don't worry about anything.'

Rosemary made a significant gesture, aware of the bleeding.

'And I can do something about that,' Tessa said practically, as she took some pads from a cupboard. 'How old are you?'

'Thirty-three.'

'Just let's take your blood pressure.' Tessa wound the cuff of the sphygmomanometer around Rosemary's upper arm. The pressure was low, the pulse soft and small.

'My blood pressure's always low,' Rosemary murmured, trying to fight the weakness and the intermittent severe pain, wretched at being denied the reunion with Giles, whom she had not seen before he left for Singapore.

Tessa looked down at her patient and said quietly, 'I'm sorry, but I must ask you this: Is there any possibility that you might be miscarrying?'

For the first time faint colour stole into the pale cheeks.

'No—oh, *no!* Not even a remote possibility.' She added with almost appealing naïvety, 'Giles and I are engaged—not lovers. I have such heavy periods, but I didn't expect this . . . I only finished a day or two ago.'

Tessa struggled to overcome her own vulnerability and involvement with the situation.

'Have you a doctor?'

'No . . . I haven't lived in Cheltenham very long, and have a job and a flat there. I'm a medical secretary,' she added.

'And like everyone in the medical profession, neglect yourself,' Tessa commented with a half-smile. So *that* accounted for Giles being in the district, raced her thoughts. Yet why hadn't he gone straight to Cheltenham?

'I suppose so.' Rosemary sighed deeply. 'I didn't want to start anything I couldn't finish before Giles came home,' she went on, as though the facts were vital and being able to impart them, a relief. 'He and I met in Oxford. I worked in the practice where he was a locum. He'd broken away from his brother's practice in London and didn't want to rush into anything. His father's health had been causing anxiety—'she broke off apologetically. 'You probably know all this.'

Tessa said, 'No; Paul introduced your fiancé this evening.' That, she thought, was true.

'Ah . . . I found just the kind of job I wanted in Cheltenham and Giles and I agreed that when he got back from Singapore we'd marry and settle in the area if the right practice was available.'

Tessa's heart seemed to miss a beat. So Giles' comment, 'I might take you up on that', when Paul had suggested a partnership, had been significant.

Rosemary continued and, observing, assessing, Tessa knew that she was in a highly emotional state, her voice unsteady, 'I knew that Giles was going to look Paul up before seeing me on his return . . . I manoeuvred things so that I could deliver an important medical report to a doctor in Tewkesbury . . . I rang Paul's house and his housekeeper gave me this address.' There was faint agitation in her voice as she added, 'I wanted to surprise him.' Even as she spoke, she gave a little spasmodic groan and clutched her stomach.

Tessa said with quiet resolution, 'I want to get you into The Meadows Nursing Home—no, don't protest until you've heard what I have to say. You're losing far too much, and you have pain, which needs a thorough investigation. You can do nothing in your present condition, let alone travel back to Cheltenham. I'd like my father to see you—he specialises in gynaecology and is very well known at The Meadows.'

'But—'

'You may only need to be there a night, and in the long run it will save you time and effort. There are many minor things and, this way, we shall know exactly what we're dealing with.' Tessa spoke on a note of cheerfulness. She managed to add, 'And your fiancé will be on the spot.'

Rosemary knew she had very little option and that what Tessa said was right.

'I feel such a—a *mess*,' came the sighing apology.

'That's the least of our worries,' Tessa assured her. 'You'll soon be properly taken care of, and in a nice clean bed.' It was strange, she thought, how in that short while she felt protective towards this frail, distraught patient.

'I *can't* see Giles like this!'

Tessa consoled her by gently removing the soiled clothes and putting her into a white gown, finally wrapping her in a red blanket.

'Now you can see anyone,' she said sympathetically. 'I know how you feel, but this is the best and only thing to do.'

Rosemary put out a hand in a frightened gesture.

'Do you—do you think I've got anything—nasty?'

Tessa said swiftly, 'Good gracious, no, but I can't make any specific diagnosis at this stage. My father will do that when he's examined you.'

'You've been so kind. I don't know what I should have done if all this had happened anywhere else.' Rosemary's voice trailed away, then, 'Could I see Giles now?'

Tessa nodded. She felt that she'd had a local anaesthetic which was wearing off now that she had fulfilled her professional role.

'I'll fetch him, and arrange with the nursing home. We can get you there in the car; it's only a few minutes away.'

Giles was in the drawing room with Adrian, Letty and Paul. He got to his feet and reached the door as Tessa entered it. She gave him the facts, as imparted by one doctor to another; otherwise, they might have been strangers. Only years of training enabled her to play her part so skilfully.

But even as she spoke, nothing could wipe out the memory of his words, *'Have dinner with me next week.'* And all the time he was engaged. Nothing wrong with that, but why couldn't he have *told* her? Why the secrecy, particularly as the fact would automatically and swiftly come to light? Nothing added up, or made sense. But she never forgot his face as he listened to the news about Rosemary, or the strange dull tone of his voice as he said, 'I'll go to her . . . thank you for all you've done.' It was as though they had become two puppets worked by invisible strings. He hesitated for a second, then hurried away.

Tessa enlisted her father's aid. He seemed suddenly to be a tower of strength as she asked him if he would make the arrangements with the nursing home. They went out into the hall together.

Adrian noticed that, when in doubt, Tessa always called him 'Daddy'; at other, more carefree times he was 'Adrian'.

'You'll see her tomorrow?' she asked.

'Of course . . . leave it to me. I'll have a word with Matron.' He gave a half-smile. 'Been quite an evening.

Karen all right?' He asked the question as he made his way to his room.

Tessa had forgotten Karen and said almost guiltily, 'As right as she ever will be.'

Giles went to Rosemary's side—strange and ill at ease. A feeling almost of doom lay upon him as he faced the fact that had drummed in his brain during the past weeks: that while he loved her, he was not, and never had been, *in* love with her. Propinquity, common interests, ambitions, had set the seal on a relationship that had merely borrowed the glow of love. Looking down at her then, he felt as he imagined a brother might have felt towards a sister to whom he was devoted, hating to see her in pain, and so vulnerable. But there was a raw wound in his heart as he thought of Tessa, and the icy contempt in her eyes as she had earlier dismissed him from that very room.

Rosemary raised her arms and buried her face against his shoulder as she cried, 'This isn't how I imagined things. I hated not seeing you today!' She explained how she came to be there and he drew back awkwardly, taking her hand in his.

'And I hate seeing you like this,' he said gently but evasively.

'I don't want to go into a nursing home. But—'

'Tessa's right,' he assured her.

'Tessa?' she echoed. Surprised by the Christian name, she looked at him questioningly.

'She's a great friend of Paul's and there was no question of any formality.'

'Oh!' Rosemary smiled. 'She's been so kind, so helpful.' Embarrassment touched her. 'I'm so sorry to have dragged you into all this.'

'Thank heaven you were here,' Giles said gratefully.

She sighed and nodded. Then, 'How's your father? I can't believe you're *home*! It's seemed so long—two whole months.'

To Giles it was completely unreal. They were in Tessa's consulting room—Tessa, who had lingered in his thoughts like some haunting melody during the past years, until he told himself that he was behaving like an adolescent schoolboy. Many times he had been tempted to look her up in the Medical Register, but was loath to risk smashing the illusion. When asking Rosemary to marry him, he firmly believed that he had laid the ghost of that night, and stilled the echo of his own prophetic words. Now he allowed his gaze to wander around the room, which was larger than the one at Chestnut Cottage, and more fully equipped. The walls were off-white, and the spacious alcove where Rosemary lay on the examining couch was arched and screened by doors that opened centrally and now stood ajar. He could visualise Tessa sitting at her desk which stood in the centre of the room, the patients' chair facing her in order that the light from a latticed window might fall at just the right angle. A bowl of roses adorned a bookcase, together with photographs of her parents. There was nothing cold or clinical about it, and he rightly guessed that she deplored the sick being treated as numbers on an assembly line, and made to feel intruders.

'I may only have to stay in a night,' said Rosemary, after what seemed a long silence. She felt uneasy and embarrassed, separation seeming to have built an imaginary wall between them.

'Precautionary,' he suggested, 'but you're in no fit condition to return to your flat in any case. This way you'll be checked out throughly.' He was grateful to be concentrating on the medical aspect, unable to think of the right things to say otherwise.

'Oh, I'm so glad you're here,' she whispered, feeling weak and near to tears. 'You'll come to see me?'

He patted her hand. 'And take you home,' he assured her.

'And will you get in touch with Dr Warren; tell him what's happened, and that I'll be back at work as soon as possible?' There was anxiety in her shaken voice. Suddenly she remembered, 'I haven't any night things—nothing *with* me.'

'I'll run over to the flat and collect all you need,' he promised, calming her. 'Don't worry.'

Tessa came in at that moment, saying comfortingly, 'I've packed all the things you'll want tonight—and I assure you it isn't the first time my nightdresses have appeared at The Meadows!' she added. 'You're booked in and my father will see you tomorrow.' She went to Rosemary's side as Giles moved away. 'I take it,' she said to him crisply, 'that you would like to see your fiancée in, and drive to the nursing home with us.'

Rosemary looked at Giles with wide, unconsciously pleading, eyes.

He said, 'Thank you—yes.'

'Then we'll go.'

Tessa helped Rosemary off the couch and draped the blanket expertly around her, noticing the solitaire diamond engagement ring that momentarily caught the sun and flashed a myriad colours in sparkling light. She raised her gaze and looked straight into Giles' eyes with penetrating cynicism.

They drove the short distance to The Meadows in silence, and there Rosemary was thankful to be taken over by a welcoming Sister-in-Charge, and to sink gratefully into a wheelchair which awaited her. She looked up at Tessa, her eyes filling with tears. 'Thank you for everything,' she murmured, then whispered to Giles, 'I'll see you tomorrow.' As she spoke she raised her face for his kiss, and he bent swiftly and touched her cheek.

'I'll ring a little later,' Tessa promised as she turned away.

Rosemary's gaze was fixed on Giles; she was struggling not to cry. It wasn't either the pain or the weakness in that moment, but the bitter disappointment of having his homecoming ruined, and the strange unhappy feeling that he had been ill at ease. The wheelchair moved away.

The magical summer night registered as Tessa got back into the car. There was a stillness and an ever-changing light from the sunset which held a breathless beauty, and bathed the old streets and magnificent Abbey in a crimson glow. How many years had passed since she and Giles had previously sat in that car alone together; passion, desire, like a flame between them? The silence was tense, and when he broke it the impact was as great as thunder.

'I *must* see you next week,' he said demandingly.

Tessa's heart seemed to hurt as she retorted, her flashing glance icy, 'There's no reason whatever to do that; your life is of no interest to me.'

CHAPTER TWO

To Giles, Tessa's words came like a whiplash, and he rapped out, 'You can't possibly make such a judgment without knowing the facts.'

'I wasn't *given* the facts,' she retorted. 'You had plenty of time.'

With that she swung the car into the short entrance to River Bank and braked fiercely, opening her door and getting out before he had time to comment. But his presence, his authority, stopped her from running ahead, as he drew her gaze to his, anger, frustration, passion, darkening his eyes, his voice commanding as it broke the electric silence. 'I repeat what I said three years ago: This is not the end.' He added on a quieter note, 'I won't come in. Make my apologies to your parents, and tell Paul I'll ring him . . . Good night, Tessa.' With that he walked away.

For a second she stood there, shaken, suffocated by emotion that was a mixture of desire and fury, because he made her feel that she had been precipitate and unreasonable. Absurd, she insisted angrily. He was an attractive philanderer, and she'd been foolish enough —*weak* enough—to . . . she almost choked with humiliation. 'This is not the end', indeed! The nerve of the man! The conceit, and disloyalty to Rosemary.

Paul came out of the house at that second and she took a deep breath to regain her composure, saying swiftly, 'Giles said he'd ring you. He didn't feel like—'

Paul cut in, 'I thought he'd go back to the hotel . . .

unfortunate business. I wonder why he didn't tell us he was engaged, although there hasn't been much time for any serious exchange of confidences.'

'You can hardly keep an engagement quiet for long,' Tessa commented, her voice sharp.

'Not a question of *that*,' Paul put in loyally. 'How is she?'

'A severe case of menorrhagia (heavy periods and loss between them), obviously low blood pressure and a general nervous tension. Anaemic, too. Adrian's seeing her tomorrow. We're lucky to have a place like The Meadows.'

'Probably something simple,' Paul said a trifle vaguely because his thoughts were elsewhere, as he added, 'You like Giles?'

'I hardly know him,' Tessa returned evasively.

'If he could join me,' Paul went on, 'it would be ideal. And with Rosemary living in Cheltenham, as he told me, what could be simpler?' There was a sudden silence before he asked, 'Why do you look so sceptical?'

'Business and friendship—'

He made an airy gesture. 'No problems there . . . I thought you and he were hitting it off splendidly.'

'*I'm* not contemplating taking him as a partner,' she flashed back. 'He's certainly a very attractive man.'

He grinned his agreement. 'A great hit with the women.'

'I can well imagine.' Tessa felt irritable. 'Give the matter some thought, that's all.'

'I've already done so.' He looked stubborn, and studied her intently, his expression changing as he said, 'When am I going to have my answer? Waiting is nerve-racking.'

She replied swiftly, 'I don't want to rush into marriage.'

'Rush?' I asked you to marry me three months ago!'

Tessa gave a little troubled sigh. Where the prospect of marrying him had been a distinct possibility, now the whole idea seemed alien, as though her life and future had suddenly been thrown into the melting pot.

'I know, Paul,' she murmured gently. 'Bear with me a little longer.'

'At least,' he said wryly, 'you haven't turned me down.' His gaze deepened. 'You look upset—*are* you?'

'It's hardly been a relaxing evening,' she reminded him. The excuse was feeble, and she knew it, because emergencies were part of her professional life.

But he said immediately, 'Thoughtless of me . . . thank you for all you've done. My friendship with Giles has always gone deep, despite the recent lack of communication. It isn't always those you see most of with whom you're closest.'

Tessa nodded, knowing he was right.

'You're a dear.' She put a hand on his arm as they walked into the house. Giles' ghost seemed to be standing in the hall, his voice echoing hauntingly. There had been the excitement of newly-awakened emotion, the thrill of anticipation. Why couldn't he have told her he was going to be married? Why the pretence? On sober reflection, she was not so naïve as to have *imagined* the dark passion in his eyes, or the tension that gave every word and look significance. Well, she thought with feminine contrariness, she had left him in no doubt of her reactions, and now she made the resolution to shut him out of her thoughts.

Paul said suddenly, and as though he had just come to a decision, 'I shall suggest that Giles comes to stay with me in case Rosemary's condition necessitates her remaining at The Meadows. We'd not had time to discuss his plans.'

Tessa didn't speak. They joined Adrian and Letty, together with a few close friends, and went into the dining room where a cold buffet had been provided by Mrs Dewsbury, the general factotum at River Bank, who took all the household responsibilities from Letty's shoulders and worked as though running her own home. A nine-to-four daily, named Ethel, helped her, both prepared to do 'anything' for the family. They had worked there for ten years.

Surgery the following morning slid Tessa back into normality. She had seen two patients at home before arriving at River Bank and greeted Adrian, professionally pleased with herself.

'The Rosemary Wyatt case,' Adrian began. 'Any points you'd like to mention? Fill me in.'

Tessa valued these sessions with her father; they could disagree, argue, congratulate, but never lose sight of the close friendship they enjoyed, and which cemented their relationship. His skill and experience fortified her and his confidence inspired her to have confidence in herself.

'Just the feeling that this isn't merely a case of disfunctional menstrual bleeding; but not having given her a pelvic examination, I can't make any judgments.' A sensation of unease surged over her as she added, her body heating, 'Nothing to do with any IUD—' As she spoke, she heard again Rosemary's almost naïve words, 'Giles and I are engaged—not lovers'. She didn't want the fact to be important, or to dwell on it, and added, 'Let's hope she may only need a D & C . . .' She went on, without knowing why, 'She's a very pleasant person and there's something a little old-fashioned about her.'

'I can't imagine Giles Rutherford with a hard, sophisticated type—even though I've only just met him.'

Tessa had reached the door and looked back at Adrian as he sat down at his desk. 'Not an easy man to assess,' she observed. 'Shall I tell Mrs Wallace to begin surgery?'

'Do. Oh, and would you give old Mrs Railton a call? I promised Nurse Humber I'd look in, but with Miss Wyatt to see I'll be thrown out of my schedule.'

Tessa gave an indulgent little chuckle. Mrs Railton was senile, of happy disposition, and lived in a rambling old house near Overbury, often going back to bed at eleven in the morning, fully dressed, quite sure it was night! She had also been known to pour fruit salad and cream over her chicken casserole, to say nothing of putting on five pairs of stockings when the nurse's back was turned and she could get at them. In a generous mood, she would insist on giving five-pound notes instead of ones, because they were 'prettier'. And when the chiropodist called, she would often be surprised because she had *two* feet, and think it was something to celebrate. She wouldn't remember Tessa, but would be delighted to see her. The prospect of the visit lightened Tessa's mood.

Giles telephoned at ten o'clock. He had already spoken to Rosemary, who had slept reasonably well. Tessa said in a professional tone, 'What can I do for you?'

'Would it be possible for you to give me some idea of the time your father will be seeing Rosemary today?'

'As near eleven as possible.'

'Is there any hope of her being able to return to her flat today?' He sounded agitated as though a vital issue were at stake.

Tessa said shortly, 'I can't give you any information at this stage—you know the routine as well as I do. But a rest would be very beneficial, although I can imagine how anxious you are for her to leave the nursing home.'

'It isn't just a question of that.' His voice was low.

Tessa was acutely conscious of him, her nerves taut, her heart quickening its beat, but she said swiftly, 'If you'll excuse me, I'm just starting surgery.'

'Thank you again.' He rang off.

She sat there staring unseeingly at the calendar on her desk. Yesterday he had been just a name and a memory. Now, today, he was disturbing her peace of mind and fragmenting her life. She told herself that her one hope was that he would leave the district, and if he went to the Antipodes it would not be too far away!

Rosemary, in the meantime, lay back against the pillows in a comfortable room looking out over the fields to the river. The flooding and pain had lessened and she no longer felt that she was about to faint, while a little of the peace of The Meadows had already brushed off on her, bringing with it an escape from responsibility. She looked around her at the white walls and the cheerful flowered curtains, the material being duplicated on the easy chair covers. Despite the circumstances, she was grateful to be there. Nothing was demanded of her in these escapist moments as she waited for Tessa's father to arrive.

Sister Allan—a dark-haired, Charlotte Brontë type girl—came in and stood smiling down at her.

'Dr Lane is on his way, and Dr Tessa telephoned; she's coming in after midday.'

'I shall be going home later on?' It was a statement rather than a question. Giles had said that he would be ready to drive her back to Cheltenham at any time. She had left her car at River Bank, so that transport didn't present any problems. He had also said he would be in to see her later on. He had sounded full of solicitude, and she had overcome the depression of the previous evening, adjusting to the fact that the situation had placed them both at a disadvantage. All reunions, in the most propitious circumstances, could be a strain.

'We'll see what the doctor says before making any plans.'

At that moment the door opened and Adrian came in, bringing an air of friendly reassurance as he greeted her, and sat down beside the bed.

'I interrupted the party last evening,' Rosemary apologised. 'Your daughter was wonderful.'

Adrian's smile concealed his pride. His professional eye was taking in every detail of Rosemary's face and expression, aware of her pallor and dark-rimmed eyes.

'We'd be lost if we didn't have any interruptions,' he assured her. 'Feeling a little better this morning?' He stood up as he spoke, glanced at Sister and walked into the adjoining bathroom to wash his hands, as he added, 'We'll have a look at you.'

The examination was thorough in every detail, internal as well as external, and when it was over and Sister had left, Adrian sat down again beside her, aware of the apprehension in Rosemary's eyes and feeling a fatherly sympathy for her as he said, 'It's a case of fibroids, which accounts for the heavy loss and recent flooding, the pain—'

She nodded and looked immediately relieved.

'It will mean an operation,' he said gently.

'Yes; I realise.' Her knowledge as a medical secretary filled in the gaps.

'You're young for this, but I advise it being done as

soon as possible. You don't want your life made a misery . . . What I would like is for you to remain here for at least a week. You need the rest and you're anaemic, your blood pressure is low . . . I want some tests done. If you're here it can all fit in with a minimum of effort.' He gave her a reassuring smile. 'Then we can operate.'

Rosemary gasped, 'You mean next week?' All she could think of was Giles and how he would feel.

'The sooner the better. You don't want a recurrence of last night.'

'It's a general anaesthetic,' she protested, suddenly fearful. 'I've never had an operation before.'

'Operations are nothing today!'

'I *know*. Isn't it silly? I'm always dealing with people and their operations, too.'

'Ah,' he said with understanding, 'it's very different when it happens to be you—or someone close to you.' He looked away for a second and then back to meet her inquiring eyes as he said, 'There's just one thing . . . I have to tell you that in the unlikely event of your needing a hysterectomy—'

She echoed the word as though it burned her tongue.

'You're talking in terms of formality?'

He evaded the word by saying, 'Any such operation would be done there and then.'

Rosemary said swiftly, 'Patients have to sign a consent form before operations, don't they, anyway?'

'Yes—surgeons can't help a patient with one hand tied!' He added, 'Equally, the patient must be put in the picture—that's essential.'

Rosemary nodded, but closed her mind against any dramatic diagnosis.

'I do understand,' she said, not wishing to dwell on the matter. 'You'll operate.'

'If that is your wish.'

'Oh, it is.'

Adrian held out his hand and shook hers. 'I'll look in tomorrow,' he promised. His manner was encouraging, his tall figure, as he got to his feet, dignified, giving an air of authority which inspired trust and confidence. His smile suggested that all would be well, but he hesitated, seemed about to add something, then walked to the door.

'Dr Tessa's coming in to see me,' Rosemary told him, depression vanishing. 'I'm wearing her nightdress!'

Adrian smiled again, then the door closed behind him.

Alone, Rosemary felt the weight of events. An operation caused an inevitable upheaval. Dr Warren would have to find temporary help, while her plans and Giles' would be interrupted, her immobility a handicap. She was grateful that he was a doctor and would appreciate the case without explanations. The thought of him made the day seem hotter, bringing a nervous tension, even agitation. What had he in mind for the future? And the date of their wedding? So many things to discuss . . .

A knock at the door made her jump and Giles came in a second later, followed by a nurse bringing coffee.

'Ah,' he said as she set the tray down, flashing her an appreciative smile, 'just what the doctor ordered!'

Nurse Briggs decided that he was 'smashing'.

Rosemary, shy, aware anew of Giles' attraction and effortless charm, exclaimed after the door shut, 'Oh, darling, I thought we'd never be alone together! I've missed you so *much*!'

He stooped and kissed her upturned face with affection, drawing away from her lips and then busying himself with the coffee cups. He was aware of her frailty, and the effort she was making to appear bright.

'It's been a long while . . . I didn't think Father would pull through.' He handed her a coffee cup, took his own, and sat down in the armchair nearest the bed. 'Now tell me what Dr Lane had to say about you.' His voice was concerned.

She gave him the facts, feeling a little bleak and disappointed by his greeting. 'It's the last thing I wanted *now*—just when you're home. Spoiling everything!'

Giles' heart sank. The talk he had intended having immediately on his return was out of the question now. He could only go along with the situation until she was well again. Pretence was foreign to him, and playing a part an anathema.

'The only important thing is your health,' he said lamely. 'You ought not to have let things go.'

'I deluded myself that it would improve, and with your coming home—' She made a little appealing gesture. 'We always seem to do the wrong things when we're most anxious to do the right.'

He said with feeling, 'How true that is . . . but now you know what's wrong—' As he sat there he realised that he was reluctant even to go into any diagnosis, or enlarge on the possibilities of that already made. Frankness and intimacy were lost in his own guilt because he had only sympathy to offer, rather than involvement. It was impossible to be natural; he could not live up to her expectations, and he knew she was waiting for a demonstration of his love for her.

'What are your plans?' There was a note of appeal in her voice.

'We'll go into all that when you're fit again,' he said vaguely. 'I shall remain at the hotel. Paul rang me this morning and wanted me to stay with him.'

Rosemary looked eager. 'That would be a splendid idea.'

'I prefer the freedom of the Bell. I can always accept his hospitality from time to time, without intruding. You'll like Paul; and he hasn't changed a bit.'

She asked tentatively, 'Are you still considering settling in this area, or have you changed your mind? You know I don't mind where we live—I can always let the flat.'

Her words struck a note of gentle irony as he reflected that she was a fine character, genuine, generous and loyal; and he knew with near-desperation that she loved him deeply, and that he had never been *in* love with her. Separation had crystallised the fear that haunted him before he went away, the folly of his mistake appalling him. On several occasions he had almost taken the coward's way out and written breaking off the engagement. It would have been so easy, but he cared too much for her and his own integrity to avail himself of that escape.

'I'd like to stay in Gloucestershire,' he admitted, recalling Paul's spontaneous offer, which would have delighted him had his relationship with Rosemary been a stable one. As it was, he was aware of his invidious position. 'But that can be settled later on, when you're better.'

A knock interrupted them and Tessa stood on the threshold, saying apologetically as she saw Giles, 'I'm sorry—I'll come back later.'

'Oh, no,' insisted Rosemary, 'please stay.'

Giles got to his feet, studying Tessa intently. She looked cool and attractive in her striped blue-and-white dress, her hair shining. She gave him a brief acknowledgment and sat down in the upright chair by the bed.

Rosemary reiterated her thanks for Tessa's help the previous night and expressed her anxiety over getting her own things, since she was not allowed to leave The Meadows.

'I told you,' Giles said patiently, 'that I'd go to the flat and bring all you need.' His smile was reassuring. 'Just make a list.'

Tessa looked from face to face and without professional assessment realised, almost with a pang, that Rosemary had a fragile beauty which awakened a protective instinct.

'I must see you next week.' Giles' words insinuated themselves, bringing a shattering emotion, and involuntarily her gaze was drawn to his in a direct, inescapable look, which held memories of the brief hours they had spent together. Swiftly, nervously, she turned her head and concentrated on Rosemary, saying with a rash impetuosity, 'It's my day off. I could easily go to Cheltenham for you and attend to it all.'

The moment the words were uttered she regretted them, not wanting to be drawn further into any personal relationship.

Rosemary protested, 'That would seem such an imposition—'

'The address and the key,' Tessa interrupted briskly. It struck her that Rosemary must surely have friends in the district, and as though reading her thoughts, Rosemary said, 'I only moved to Cheltenham just before Giles went away. Giles and I had talked of settling in the area, and there was a job that was exactly right. I haven't anyone who could help me, I'm afraid. I deliberately didn't want to make friends until Giles and I could do so together.'

Tessa nodded her understanding and flashed Giles a

faintly critical look. 'You seem to have been a very nomadic doctor,' she observed.

Giles' expression was resistant.

'Amicably severing my partnership with my brother because I didn't want to work in London for the rest of my life, and taking a locum job in Oxford for my own convenience prior to finding a permanent base is hardly that,' he returned concisely. 'My father's illness hasn't facilitated matters.'

'But we love the idea of being in Gloucestershire—don't we, darling?' Rosemary put in swiftly. 'Although it doesn't matter where one lives . . . I'd move *anywhere*. We were just talking about it all when you came in. I've spoilt things,' she added wretchedly.

Giles took command, his nerves taut.

'I suggest that I drive you over to Cheltenham,' he said forcefully to Tessa. 'I know the flat and can give some assistance.' He was impatient of fuss.

'That,' said Rosemary with obvious relief, 'would make me feel much less guilty. And not be quite so much trouble.' She looked at Tessa hopefully.

Tessa wanted to refuse, but knew that having said she was free for the day, she had no alternative but to agree.

'Thank you,' she said. 'If you could pick me up at the cottage at two-thirty.' Her voice was businesslike.

'You don't live at River Bank?' Rosemary looked surprised, and Tessa explained.

Rosemary gave a little wistful sigh. 'My parents are dead—they died when I was fourteen. An aunt brought me up after then . . . *she* died earlier this year.'

It struck Tessa forcefully that Rosemary was alone and that Giles must, in consequence, mean more to her than ever as a result. The fact seemed depressing.

Rosemary asked impulsively, 'Will you be my doctor?

I mean for as long as I'm in Cheltenham? And after the operation? She hastened, 'I'd come to *you* unless it was an emergency.'

'We do try to keep to about a three-mile radius,' Tessa temporised.

'Oh, *please*—' Rosemary looked agitated, the strain of the morning taking its toll.

'Very well,' promised Tessa, feeling that Giles' gaze was upon her almost challengingly, his silence unnerving.

Rosemary sighed and sank deeper into the pillows. She felt hot and exhausted, and Tessa, getting up from the chair, said, 'You've had enough—'

'I haven't made out a list—' The words were agitated.

Tessa dismissed the idea.

'Just the keys,' Giles said quietly.

Rosemary took them from her handbag. 'Can't you have lunch together?' she suggested, looking from face to face.

There was an almost electric silence which Tessa broke by saying hurriedly, 'I'm seeing a friend—thank you all the same.' The statement was true inasmuch as she had promised to call on Paul at his house, The Hollows, near Barton Road. But lunch had not been mentioned. She put her hand on Rosemary's and hurried from the room, murmuring, as she glanced at Giles, 'I'll see you at two-thirty.'

She went out into the bright sunshine as though moving from one world to another, turmoil making her feel churned up and self-critical. Somehow she had allowed herself to be drawn into Rosemary's affairs, her natural sympathy and desire to help almost a vice, she argued. And why hadn't she suggested meeting Giles at River Bank? Why the cottage? Except that it was associated in her mind with him, no matter how great her chagrin.

She called at The Hollows, but Paul was out, so she left a message with Randall, his general factotum who ran the house with the aid of Mrs Cross, a daily, and felt a mixture of relief and disappointment as she got back in her car and returned home. The telephone rang almost immediately, and an irate voice which she recognised as belonging to a matriarchal Mrs Warleigh said, 'It's vital that I see you. It's about my daughter.' She emphasised the word *daughter*, although Tessa knew Dulcie well and, indeed, the whole family.

'Is Dulcie ill?' asked Tessa, not put off by the aggressive tone of voice.

'That depends what you mean by ill . . . I want to see you.'

'It's my day off, Mrs Warleigh. If anyone is ill, then that's a different matter. If not, I suggest you make an appointment—'

'You'd do well to see me, Dr Tessa. It's a serious matter,' Mrs Warleigh added darkly. 'For you.'

'I don't respond to threats,' Tessa emphasised coldly. 'But I'm prepared to see you at five o'clock—no, make it five-thirty, here.'

'Five-thirty,' came the short retort, and the line went dead.

Tessa put down the receiver. Mrs Warleigh had never been her favourite patient. She wrote in her day-book: Mrs Warleigh, 5.30. It was a good thing to have an appointment to hasten her return from Cheltenham, she thought.

Giles arrived punctually at two-thirty, and she was ready at the front door, handbag in hand, taking the key out of the lock. She didn't want him to come in.

'It looks as though we're in for a storm,' he said, indicating the black clouds low against the previously blue sky. The bright sunlight had dimmed and there was an ominous silence, different from that which normally lay over the countryside. 'Hadn't you better bring a coat—mac?'

She fumed inwardly at his naturalness and a certain suggestion of intimate solicitude, and retorted contrarily, 'I seldom bother with coats . . . I'm not afraid of a little rain. It would be a pleasure, in fact!'

He made no comment, merely stood aside as she locked the front door and walked with her in silence to his car.

Rosemary's flat was in a converted Georgian building, near the Promenade, with its graceful hanging baskets and double avenue of horse-chestnuts, luxurious shops and Regency terrace converted into Municipal Offices. Lawns and flower-beds adorned the town, giving it a certain elegance which neither time nor traffic had wholly destroyed.

As Tessa expected, the flat itself was in perfect order: charming, artistically furnished, with pastel shades predominating. It was a simple matter to find the necessary garments and toiletries because each was in its rightful place; drawers and cupboards nearly stacked, so that even in the dark one could find a given article in a given place. Tessa had made a list, and put everything necessary on the bed.

'A case,' said Giles. 'Now where would cases be kept?'

He and Tessa had exchanged only cursory remarks since their arrival, but now the task was almost completed, they looked at each other, aware of the incongruousness of the position.

Tessa, indiscreetly, exclaimed, 'If anyone had told me yesterday that I'd be here, like this, today . . .' She stopped and involuntarily their eyes met as they had done the previous evening. There was no escape, and she felt emotion slowly building up, slowly, inexorably and almost with fear, as she realised with a shattering certainty that she loved him; and where, over the years, she had remembered him as a woman might remember a film star, now she was faced with a grim reality. This was no fantasy, no illusion. He was standing before her, looking down at her, and it took all her strength not to fling herself into his arms.

'Tessa!' He called her name on a note of alarm.

She sat down on the bed, swirling momentarily in a mixture of pain and ecstasy.

'It's so hot,' she managed to exclaim. 'I think you were right about a storm.' She didn't want to look at him, and yet felt impelled to do so, and the dark intensity in his eyes, the almost brooding regret, made her catch at her breath because it would have been so easy to believe that he shared her feelings. And out of that wishful thinking came the brutal fact: *He was going to marry Rosemary*. What madness; what havoc love could awaken in its craving to be reciprocated! She despised her own weakness and managed to say briefly, 'The case . . . probably the top of the hall cupboard,' she added.

'Tessa?' Again he spoke her name, but this time in a low hoarse voice that made her heart thump. 'I can't say what I'd intended—'

She got to her feet and moved ahead of him into the hall, throwing her words over her shoulder because she dared not meet his gaze. 'I've already made it plain that we have nothing to say to each other, Giles . . . now let's get these things together. I have a patient to see.'

He followed her and stood barring her way, looking at her with a fierce intensity, a dogged determination.

'But there is one thing I *can* say,' he exclaimed challengingly. 'I intend to accept Paul's offer to join him in his practice. My mind is made up.'

CHAPTER THREE

TESSA heard Giles' words with a mixture of fear, annoyance and grudging relief. The initial shock over, she said coolly, 'Your future has nothing to do with me. Circumstances have drawn me into your immediate affairs and I'll look after Rosemary professionally. There the matter ends. As far as I'm concerned you are a man about to be married. I suggest you remember that, instead of indulging in innuendo which is thoroughly disloyal.' The words rushed out, ironically hurting her as much as they hurt him. She waited for his protestations, but all he said was, 'I'll make you reverse that judgment, Tessa. Explanations are impossible at the moment.'

'There's nothing to explain,' she retorted loftily. 'We're two strangers whose paths happen to have crossed.'

He drew her gaze to his with a powerful determination, making it impossible for her to avoid him.

'We could never be strangers and you know it,' he said hoarsely.

She was trembling, overwhelmed by his attraction and at the mercy of her emotion. She wanted to retaliate, to think of a glib contradiction, but her brain wouldn't function.

A gleam of satisfaction came into Giles' eyes that touched the edge of triumph. He moved forward and silently opened the cupboard door, found a case and brought it down.

Tessa packed it as though in a trance. The first clap of

thunder reverberated ominously and she felt that the gathering storm reflected her mood. Rain slashed down like rods, glistening in the dazzling forked lightning.

When the case was finally packed, Giles opened a wardrobe door and found a white mackintosh.

'You'll need this,' he said quietly. 'It looks like being a long storm, or we could wait.'

She said hastily, 'I want to get back.' But she slid into the garment he held out for her, aware of the touch of his hands as he smoothed them over her shoulders, grateful that she and Rosemary were the same size.

'What about you?' she asked involuntarily.

'I'm sure there's an umbrella somewhere . . . you'll need it for your hair, anyway.'

She flashed at him, 'You think of everything!'

He looked down at her reflectively. 'And you have only tunnel vision,' he quipped, finding an umbrella.

The storm gathered momentum, the thunder bomb-like, splitting the heavens with atomic violence. The car was only across the road from the flat, but already the pavements were awash, the road dangerous after a period of prolonged heat. Giles held the umbrella and took Tessa's arm. She made no protest, grateful for his protection, a surge of love robbing her of animosity for those brief moments as he helped her into the car and got in the driver's seat. Traffic had piled up; exhausts were puffing their acrid fumes into the humid air. He eased his way out of a tight parking space; the windscreen wipers whined, the steam blurred the windscreen and the rain danced on the bonnet of the car, blinding him.

'We should have waited,' he said.

'I must get back,' Tessa replied doggedly, his presence tormenting.

He drove expertly, manoeuvring his way through the

traffic, judging distance to an inch, until they were out in the windswept countryside, headlights necessary in the weird purple darkness through which the lightning struck with a sorcerer's magic. Rain almost immobilised them; the heat inside the car was oppressive.

When they reached the cottage courtesy forced Tessa to say, 'I'll make a cup of tea.' She found she was waiting for his answer and, despite all her conflicting thoughts, not wanting to see him go.

'That would be welcome.' They ran the short distance from the car to the front door, his umbrella useless against the wind. Once inside they breathed deeply, drawn together by the experience. Tessa's anger was spent. She was only aware of Giles' presence, and the futility of conjecture. He joined her in the kitchen, plugging in the kettle as though his being there was perfectly natural.

'Biscuits?' she asked.

'No, thank you.'

He carried the tea-tray into the sitting room a few minutes later and sat down opposite her. Silence fell, tense, pregnant with emotion that could find no expression in words. Challenge gave place to a strange and inevitable acceptance, as though all the warring elements had been lost in the storm.

'When is your patient due?' he asked quietly, putting his cup back on the tray.

'Not until five-thirty,' she admitted, adding, 'but I want to read up her notes and get a few other things done before then.' She found him unnerving and emotion flared, shattering the momentary calm. Her love for him seemed to bruise her heart and cause physical pain, making her shrink from its reality. The thought of Rosemary came back with devastating awareness.

The telephone rang and she answered it, grateful for the diversion, then, 'Paul . . . I called . . . Yes, I've been out; Giles and I—' she explained the situation. 'Dinner? I could meet you. Fairfield Manor, sevenish . . . 'Bye.' She put the receiver down and her gaze went to Giles; his eyes met hers in a long lingering look which defied escape; the memory of his invitation lying between them with renewed significance. Nervously she got to her feet and lifted the tea-tray, unable to stand the strain of sitting opposite him a minute longer.

Immediately he took the tray from her, their hands touching as he did so, the contact like a physical shock.

A few seconds later they stood together by the front door.

'I'll get back to the hospital,' he said in a flat expressionless voice. 'Thank you for your help. I shouldn't have known what to select when it came to it.'

She nodded, cringing at the banality of her words as she said, 'The storm's almost over . . . the umbrella!' As she spoke she returned to the kitchen and retrieved it from the sink.

'Thank you for the tea.' He stood there, reluctant to leave.

'Goodbye, Giles.' There was a note of dismissal in her voice.

He hesitated, looked down at her, then said with telling emphasis, '*Au revoir*, Tessa.'

She watched him, unseen, from the sitting-room window as he got into his car. What would have happened if she had encouraged him when he had said, '*I can't say what I'd intended*—'? His whole manner was disquieting and certainly not that of an engaged man. Only, she argued bitterly, of a philanderer, who wanted to marry one woman and flirt with another. Always conveying more than he actually felt.

The car disappeared from sight. The house seemed as empty as her heart.

Mrs Warleigh arrived promptly at five-thirty, coming in as though she were the judge and Tessa was already in the dock. She wore a coat-frock type of dress in unrelieved navy. Her hair was straight and cut in a hard line about her face which was devoid of make-up, and had a scrubbed look which was unkind to her sallow skin. Her eyes were beady and darted from one object to another with piercing criticism. If you gave Mrs Warleigh a beautiful apple, she would immediately suspect that there was a maggot at the core.

'I won't mince words, Dr Tessa,' she began.

Tessa knew that meant a tirade. She indicated the patients' chair when they reached her consulting room, and took her place at her desk.

'Now,' she said, her voice firm, her gaze steady.

'You've been prescribing contraceptive pills to Dulcie—without my consent. That's against the law when a girl is under sixteen, and I intend to take the matter up—'

Tessa's voice rang out with authority, 'And I suggest you verify your facts before you make such an accusation. In any case, were it an emergency I would have every right to do so.'

Mrs Warleigh's mouth opened and stayed open for a fraction of a second before she exclaimed, 'So you admit it?'

'There's nothing to admit,' Tessa said icily. 'I haven't seen Dulcie since I attended her for influenza—'

'That was months ago.' The tone was suspicious.

'Exactly. I've neither heard nor spoken to her since.'

An expression of fear crept into the hard accusing eyes, and a little of the bombast vanished.

'What makes you suspect that she is on the pill?' Tessa spoke with a calm enquiry.

'She's behaving strangely, is secretive. No appetite —generally out of sorts.'

Tessa looked thoughtful. 'Oral contraceptives affect different people in different ways. Some people have no side effects whatsoever; others can't tolerate certain brands.'

'I don't approve of any of them; and I'll never allow her to take them,' came the snappy retort.

'It won't be within your jurisdiction, Mrs Warleigh, for very much longer.'

'I'm her *mother*! She'll do as I say.'

'Have you talked to her about the matter?'

'She knows my views; I've made them clear enough.'

Tessa thought, 'Too clear', but made no comment.

'This isn't the easiest time of a girl's life,' she said with understanding. 'Their emotions—'

'Emotion!' Mrs Warleigh spluttered. 'She's a *child*, and if I thought that she'd been prescribed the pill—' Dark anger filled her eyes.

'The Progesterone-only oral contraceptive can—'

But Mrs Warleigh wasn't listening.

Tessa tried again. 'Has she a particular boy-friend?'

'Not to my knowledge. She's still at *school*. *Boy-friends!*' she echoed in disgust. 'Nothing but sex these days. In *my* day—' She was in her forty-second year when Dulcie had been born—the one and only child —unwanted. With her temperament and lack of any kind of warmth, the whole process of physical love had been offensive to her. Her husband had retreated into his garden, a sad, grey little man who, nevertheless, was a successful electrical engineer, providing his wife with comfort and security, which she took as a right.

'You're still a comparatively young woman, Mrs Warleigh, and it might be a good idea if you remembered that when dealing with Dulcie. *Understand* her—' Tessa paused. 'If you're worried about her health in any way—'

'I'm suspicious,' came the confession with a certain venom. 'She keeps her drawers locked, or I'd—' She stopped, aware of Tessa's disapproving expression.

'Suspicion is a poor companion,' Tessa shot at her, 'and it won't inspire your daughter's confidence.'

'She's been brought up to obey me; taught right from wrong and the consequences of the latter. Now that *you* can't enlighten me—' Mrs Warleigh got up from her chair with a martyred air. 'Give children everything and what do you get? No gratitude—nothing but trouble!'

'And if Dulcie isn't well and isn't taking any kind of—'

'She'd come to see you,' came the harsh but logical reply.

That, thought Tessa, was true.

'Would she be able to see any other doctor?'

'No; Dulcie is my patient; registered with me, and except in an emergency—' Tessa paused. 'If I could talk to her and—'

Mrs Warleigh interrupted, 'I've *warned* her that I shall insist on her coming to you.'

There was a sudden awkward silence. The word, 'warned', told its own tale of disharmony.

Tessa looked at Mrs Warleigh with a deep penetrating gaze as she asked directly, 'Are you afraid she's pregnant? Is that what all this is really about?'

Words of protest fell from the thin lips and colour dyed the sallow cheeks.

'Pregnant!' The sound was outraged. 'At her age?'

Tessa insisted, 'Since you suspect that she might be taking the pill, pregnancy isn't so far away. She wouldn't be taking it unless—'

Again Mrs Warleigh interrupted, this time with a vehement, 'It's all revolting. To think I have even to *discuss* it!'

'The important thing is that Dulcie needs help, no matter what your opinions may be.' Tessa paused and then shot the question, 'What made you think of the pill, or the possibility of her taking it?'

'I thought of it,' came the waspish answer, 'because of all there is in the papers about it. And because I've heard—read about—the possible side effects.'

'And you came here today in the spirit of righteous indignation,' commented Tessa. 'My not being involved doesn't solve the problem. Dulcie is my patient, and if she's not well, she becomes my concern.' She leaned forward in a gentle conciliatory pose. 'Unless you're completely honest with me, I'm powerless. This is not the Dark Ages, and if there's any likelihood of Dulcie being pregnant, then we've got to think of ways and means of winning her confidence before we can even begin to help her.'

'Her *confidence*!' Mrs Warleigh changed the emphasis. '*Her* confidence? And what about my feelings in the matter? She's fifteen—a child. I didn't know anything at her age, and was all the better for it.' She got to her feet as she spoke. 'And I don't think we have anything further to discuss.'

Tessa shook her head. Mrs Warleigh's dark tormenting fear had been dragged from the cupboard and she couldn't face its hideousness, or sustain any reasonable or logical discussion. In her desperation the pill had seemed the lesser of two evils, and to attack Tessa for prescribing it, a crusade. Tessa had, in fact, become the whipping-boy.

Tessa walked to the door. 'I agree. But you know where to find me if your daughter should need me.' She paused before adding with gentleness and concern, 'You're her mother, and so much depends on your attitude; jumping to the wrong conclusions, condemning out of hand, can lead to tragedy. Dulcie may well be going through a difficult phase, both physically and mentally.'

'Thank you,' came the sharp retort, 'I don't need you to tell me how to deal with my own daughter!'

'There is one thing,' Tessa said with professional authority, 'I would suggest that you get to know her better—in the interest of you both.'

Mrs Warleigh shot her a look that could kill, but anger didn't remove the fear from her eyes as she walked haughtily from the cottage and drove away.

As Tessa shut the front door she had the presentiment of impending tragedy and made a mental note to call in at the Warleigh house on some pretext, when she could be reasonably sure that Dulcie was at home. Welcome or not.

Paul was awaiting her in the spacious hall of Fairfield Manor when she arrived that evening. A warm feeling of pleasure touched her as she saw him. He looked casually immaculate in his grey suit and white shirt. She was never quite sure about her feelings for Paul. It wasn't a case of purely platonic friendship, or the comfort of a staunch admirer in the background, but rather of being part of the life of a man who understood her needs, could flirt without giving offence, and yet leave her in no doubt as to his love for her, and desire to marry her. Equally, there was no question of her being in love with him. The word 'love' brought a painful sensation that hurt her heart, the thought of Giles tormenting her. No doubt at this moment he would be with Rosemary. He was a disruptive influence; a man who crashed into life like thunder in moonlight. She wondered, even in that second, if there was any way she could dissuade Paul from making him a partner, by adding weight to her previous argument which had already been dismissed.

'Drinks on the terrace?' he asked, and seeing her nod of approval gave their order to a passing waiter who knew him.

'I'd like a Pimm's,' Tessa said swiftly, 'it will be refreshing.'

'It's an idea,' Paul agreed. 'Make that two,' he added to the waiter.

Fairfield Manor was on the Malvern road and commanded a magnificent view of the hills. At one time the home of the Fairfields, it had been turned into a hotel on the death of Edmund Fairfield, the proceeds going mainly to the Inland Revenue. It had all the graciousness and elegance of the past, together with the benefits and comfort of modernity. A wide terrace looked over about thirty-five acres of woodland, gardens and an imposing lake where swans added to the tranquillity. The entrance hall, with its wide vast staircase, swept up to the first floor, its mullioned windows giving views over the landscape. Deep-piled carpets killed all sound and the sun streamed in, trapping the light in a golden shower and falling on antique furniture, deep armchairs upholstered in cream and gold damask, offering comfort and relaxation.

'I never come here,' said Tessa, 'without seeing it as if for the first time. It holds the magic of yesterday.' She looked towards the terrace and the illimitable views beyond, where the Malvern Hills were etched against a cloudless blue sky. And suddenly, achingly, she wanted Giles with her, and a terrible empty loneliness gripped her. Her vision blurred until she saw only his tall figure and his eyes looking into hers.

She sat down mechanically at a table immediately in front of the balustrading, Paul hovering to put her chair into position. The wooded splendour of the scene with its smooth lawns and rose arbours was lost to her until she heard his voice saying, 'Will you be joining me for dinner later on?'

She started, blinked and made a half-apologetic gesture, aware that her drink already awaited her.

'It's easy to daydream in this setting,' she explained.

He shot her a puzzled look as they sipped their Pimm's.

Tessa plunged, 'You know what I said about not mixing business with pleasure when it came to taking Giles into partnership?'

Paul jerked his head up, alert to the seriousness in her voice.

'I know,' he said in a level tone. 'I disagreed.' He had a stubborn resistance in his eyes as he added, 'As it happens, I saw Giles just before I came here. We've sealed the bargain and he's joining me. I couldn't be more pleased.'

The thought flashed through Tessa's mind that Giles must almost have gone straight from her to Paul. She forced a note of brightness into her comment, 'Then I can only share your enthusiasm . . . do you know when he and Rosemary are getting married?'

'No; it's a matter he didn't want to discuss until she's well again. For the time being, he's going to take Hill Cottage furnished.'

Tessa gasped, 'Your sister Hazel's house? But I thought it was already let?'

'It has been; the tenants go out next week and Hazel doesn't return from Spain for six months. Couldn't be better—ideal for him, and a stone's throw from The Hollow.' Paul added quietly, 'I've reached the end of my tether and he's going to help me out immediately. The one-man show isn't practical in these days, much as I've liked being on my own.'

Tessa nodded and looked sympathetic.

'You've been urging me to take a partner,' he reminded her.

'True. Possibly I'm wary of spur-of-the-moment decisions. The time factor—' She went on, not wanting to go more deeply into the question, 'But then mistakes can be made after lengthy consideration.'

'Exactly. I hope we shall make a happy foursome.'

Tessa managed to smile and asked swiftly, 'Does Rosemary know?'

'He hadn't discussed it with her, but he was going to tell her this evening. You like her?'

'Yes,' Tessa said unhesitatingly. 'She's genuine. I should say she has a fine character, but she looks as though she needs protecting.'

'Giles wouldn't like a hard, sophisticated type.'

Tessa remarked, 'The very words my father used, oddly enough. You'll like her, and she should make a good doctor's wife providing she's physically strong enough to cope.' It went through Tessa's mind that a delicate wife might well retard Giles' progress, and place on Paul an unequal work-load, in which case he would be better off on his own. There was no enmity or bitterness in the reflection, merely a natural concern.

'Probably be fighting fit when she gets over this episode. Giles and I had a talk. Doctors can never rationalise things when they are emotionally involved with the case.' Paul added earnestly, 'I want all this to work, Tessa. Giles is a fine chap and the only man I've ever felt I could confide in—or, for that matter, talk to in any depth.'

Tessa sat there, despairing, an untenable situation building up around her.

She murmured words of encouragement and a little later forced herself to eat a meal of lobster Thermidor, followed by fresh strawberries and cream, with which they had champagne. Tessa wondered if Paul had given Giles any indication that he himself wanted to marry her. Men, she thought, were more cagey than women, and were guarded about their relationships. She wished almost frantically that she could be in love with Paul; it would be so simple and ideal. In that moment she resented her love for Giles and wanted to escape from its repercussions, seeing the large lofty-ceilinged room in which they sat through a haze of regret. Chandeliers hung from the domed ceiling, with its exquisite murals; vast windows looked out over the lake, with always the Malverns keeping sentinel, and now a hazy blue in the evening light. Immaculate napery and cut-glass adorned the tables, each of which boasted a silver vase of roses. The service was excellent, enhancing the meal and creating the right atmosphere.

'We'll bring Giles and Rosemary here,' Paul said finally as they left. He spoke as though he and Tessa were already married.

Tessa flashed him a surprised look.

'Meaning that I'm taking too much for granted,' he countered instantly.

'I don't want to get too involved,' she said honestly. 'Already Rosemary wants me to be her doctor—'

'Splendid!' Paul exclaimed. 'As for not being too involved, when you decide to marry me—' He broke off and then finished with, 'As I said just now, I hope we shall make a happy foursome.'

Tessa didn't speak, but gave him a weak little smile.

'A lovely evening, anyway,' he added, not wishing to pressurise her on the subject.

The telephone was ringing as Tessa returned to the cottage a little later, and she answered it, suspecting an emergency. But to her surprise, it was Giles.

'I rather imagine that Paul will have told you I'm joining him,' he said without preamble.

'Yes.'

'Will you reserve your judgment about all this until Rosemary is better?' His words sounded solemn.

Tessa clung to her former resolution. 'I've already made it clear that your actions are no concern of mine. But since Paul is involved, I sincerely hope that he can rely on you.'

'I suggest you trust his judgment in preference to your own, Tessa.' The words came in a low but firm voice.

'It's still of no consequence. I don't know why you thought this call necessary.' She could not resist adding, 'I hope Rosemary is pleased—she won't have far to move when you're married.' She finished, 'And now if you'll excuse me . . . good night,' and replaced the receiver.

The silence around her was deep and the room filled with Giles' presence. Why should he telephone her? In twenty-four hours he had taken her life by storm, confounded all her preconceived ideas, and left her at war with herself. It was as though he were willing her to believe that some momentous happening would be taking place once Rosemary was better. She scorned the possibility as no more than a ruse to further his own flirtatious ends. All he had succeeded in doing, she told herself fiercely, was to precipitate her into marrying Paul.

Again the telephone rang and she answered it abruptly, then, 'Mrs Warleigh?'

A distracted voice cried, 'Dulcie—she's ill—'

'I'll come at once.' Tessa replaced the receiver.

Mrs Warleigh met Tessa at the door and said, making a supreme effort to be calm after her somewhat impassioned plea over the telephone, 'I think it's 'flu, Doctor. High temperature, headache . . .' She avoided Tessa's steady gaze and led the way to the bedroom with which Tessa was familiar.

'If you'll leave us, Mrs Warleigh,' Tessa said firmly.

'But—'

'I . . . don't . . . want . . . *her*—' came the muffled appeal from the bed.

Tessa waited a second until the door had closed and then moved to Duclie's side, putting a thermometer in her mouth before beginning to talk. Her temperature was a hundred and three.

'Now,' she began gently, 'I must know, Dulcie.'

'My head aches; I've got a pain—' Dulcie indicated the lower part of her stomach and then, weakly, despairingly, whispered, 'I *took* something—' She drew in a painful breath. 'I daren't tell her. But it was nearly a week ago.'

'What did you take?' Tessa asked urgently.

Dulcie shook her head. 'I don't know. A friend gave it to me . . . medicine . . . I thought it had worked. Oh, Doctor, I didn't want it to be . . . like this!'

'Why didn't you come to see me? *Why?*' groaned Tessa.

'You couldn't have helped me without my mother knowing.' The words came slowly, and with a quiet despair and inevitability.

Even while making a professional assessment, Tessa was aware of the girl's unusual beauty; the large, now dark-rimmed eyes, and pale fine skin, flushed with fever. Her hair, soft and silken, lay over the pillow like a frame. She looked eighteen.

'Gary and I went to school together; Mother didn't like him . . . we've always loved each other. We want—' the voice grew fainter, 'to get married . . . later on.'

Tessa echoed, 'You say you thought the medicine had worked?'

'Something came away . . . and it all stopped. But now . . . I'm so frightened!'

As Tessa examined her the words septic abortion were running through her mind—the embryo being expelled, leaving the placenta and membranes behind in the uterus, with the possibility of the infection spreading to the fallopian tubes and the danger of future sterility.

'The bleeding stopped,' Tessa queried, 'and then a discharge started?'

'Yes; I thought everything was all right . . . it's my *mother* . . . I couldn't tell her, talk to her.' The admission came in a desperate rush. 'She mustn't know!'

Tessa said with a grave urgency, 'I'll talk to your mother; she'll have to know, because we must get you to hospital at once.'

'No! Oh no!' Dulcie grasped Tessa's hand, panic in her eyes. Then, with a little painful gasp, she whispered, 'So . . . *ill*.' Her head dropped, and she sank into that twilight world of suffering.

'Hospital?' Mrs Warleigh exclaimed, when Tessa told her. 'There's no need whatsoever for that—'

But Tessa ignored her and hurried towards the telephone, arranging for Dulcie to be admitted as an emergency and for an ambulance to be sent immediately.

The receiver replaced, Tessa outlined the situation to Mrs Warleigh, stressing Dulcie's fears and finishing with, 'She's a very sick girl, and they'll probably have to give her a general anaesthetic for an evacuation of the uterus.'

'Pregnant? Abortion? My *daughter!*'

'You must have suspected,' Tessa said with a certain authority. 'Why didn't you send for me?'

'I came to you because of the pill. I—' Mrs Warleigh stumbled, then, 'I've no pity for her; we've always been a respectable family.'

Tessa gave her a steady, faintly contemptuous look of disgust. 'If you'll pack a few things and, since Dulcie is a minor, as next of kin you'll have to sign the consent form for anything that may be necessary to be done.'

'Go to the *hospital*?' It was a cry. 'My husband is away on business. He'll be ringing—'

Tessa ignored that and went back to Dulcie. A very short while later she had a last word with Mrs Warleigh.

'Please realise that Dulcie is very ill . . . she needs your support—'

'I don't require you to tell me how to behave to my own daughter! She'll pay for this, I promise you!'

Tessa returned home.

At midnight the door bell rang and Mrs Warleigh stood there in a state of shock.

'Dulcie's dead,' she muttered. '*Dead!*'

Tessa, in dressing gown, led the stunned woman into the sitting room.

'It was *seeing* her; hearing her . . . whisper . . . "If only you'd *understood*—"'

Tessa made a cup of tea which she sweetened, having no words of comfort to offer, because Dulcie had summed up the situation in those last tragic words.

'Something about septicop—'

'Septicopyaemia—bacteria and pus in the blood—'

Mrs Warleigh said in a flat desolate voice, 'I didn't love her, you see; I never wanted her . . . I wouldn't have Gary in the house . . . my husband said I'd drive them—' She faltered. 'I didn't expect to feel like this.' The dark beady eyes softened into remorse. 'I wished her dead when you told me.' She covered her face with her hands. 'God help me, I wished her dead. Now I don't know how to face it all . . . my husband will blame me.' She gave a shuddering sigh and gazed at Tessa as though pleading for salvation. 'You blame me—'

'It's not for me to sit in judgment,' Tessa said quietly. 'But it's always a good thing to remember that we can never get back yesterday, or retract harsh words.' She sighed, a deep sad sigh. 'It's such a tragedy. Nothing can change that.'

'My husband loved her . . .' There was desperation in the words. 'I resented the way he always defended her.'

Tessa didn't ask why this woman had sought her out at this hour: she knew. It was a question of unburdening herself of the guilt that now left her shattered and alone—bitter, hard and a stranger to love.

'Then,' Tessa said gently, 'help him to bear his grief. Nothing can bring Dulcie back, but don't let her death be altogether in vain.'

Silence fell and Tessa watched the lines of the

unattractive face relax slightly; the lips loosen their unyielding line; the eyes open a little wider, and fill with tears.

'Thank you for listening to me, Doctor. I'd no right to come here, but there was no one else, and I couldn't bear the thought of an empty house.' Mrs Warleigh got to her feet as she spoke, seeming smaller and suddenly vulnerable, as the enormity of events surged back in a spasm of renewed anguish and fear. 'Good night,' she whispered as they reached the door.

Tessa saw her into the car. 'I'll look in later on,' she said.

Mrs Warleigh nodded; there was a dumb misery about her, more pathetic than words.

CHAPTER FOUR

TESSA outlined Dulcie's case to her father just before surgery the following morning.

'Had she come to me, should I have regarded her as an emergency and put her on the pill?'

'What,' Adrian asked of no one in particular, 'constitutes an emergency?' He shook his head. 'Doctors are not clairvoyant, although they're expected to be! Contraception is preferable to conception in such cases. Nothing that either a doctor or a parent says will stop two emotionally involved youngsters sleeping together if they intend to. I don't like the pill prescribed to girls in their early teens, but it won't be any less lethal because the parent *knows*! It's one area of human relationships that you can't possibly legislate for. Preaching abstinence is justified and wise, but giving youngsters advice can sometimes be like lighting a fire with petrol! I haven't any answers. And there's no easy solution, because there are so many warring elements.' He looked at Tessa very levelly. 'Would you have put Dulcie on the pill without telling her mother?'

'With hindsight—yes. It would have saved her life.'

'Ah,' Adrian exclaimed, a faintly wry expression on his face, 'we're not asked to make judgments with hindsight, but foresight. Not so easy.'

Tessa looked at him affectionately. 'You're a wise old owl,' she said.

'Not wise enough when it comes to dealing with the Dulcies of this world.' He shook his head.

'I feel so helpless,' Tessa said sadly, 'and almost guilty.'

'That's foolish. As I've just said, we're not clairvoyant. And had she consulted you and you'd prescribed the pill, you would have been up against her mother's wrath and probable legal action . . . Now, anything urgent today?'

'I hope not. I don't want any more hospital/nursing home cases for the moment. Two in twenty-four hours are enough.'

Adrian shot her an enquiring look. 'All in a day's work, surely.'

'I don't suppose you've heard that Giles is going into partnership with Paul.' The words rushed out involuntarily.

Adrian's brows lifted in surprise.

'Why, no! That was quick, but since they're old friends . . . Glad to hear it. Paul needs help. Where should I be without *you*?' His chuckle concealed his praise.

The intercom went. Mrs Wallace was sending in the first patient, and was Dr Tessa ready to begin surgery?

Adrian and Tessa exchanged significant glances. Mrs Wallace was an excellent secretary, forty-five and of the old school, but a stickler for time; and since her assistant, Joan Risden, was on holiday, she was overworked. Mrs Wallace refused to have a temp, insisting that while she was telling a newcomer what to do, she could do it herself.

Tessa went into her consulting room, feeling curiously suspended. The vision of Giles intruded, as though he had become her shadow, his words about her reserving her judgment until Rosemary was better awakening a curiosity she was unable to stifle.

Paul accompanied Tessa to see Rosemary the day before the operation. It was ridiculous, Paul insisted, that he had not met Giles' fiancée, particularly as, inevitably, she would in future be part of his friendship with Giles.

'Giles hasn't seemed particularly eager for me to meet Rosemary,' said Paul, slightly puzzled, as he and Tessa drove to the nursing home. 'He always talks of things after her operation, as though it were some kind of turning point. Has he said anything to you?'

Tessa felt that she was in a bumpy lift.

'Very much the same.' She tried to sound casual. 'On the other hand, until she's about again, neither he nor she can plan any social life, and no one wants to meet new people in these circumstances.'

'True,' he said, a note of relief in his voice.

Paul found Rosemary an appealing person, whom he immediately liked. Her faint shyness and reticence enhanced a personality which was nevertheless extremely attractive. He was relieved to be able to talk to her, since Giles, who had arrived earlier, had retreated almost into silence and Tessa, he thought, was faintly ill at ease.

'I'm so delighted that Giles is joining you,' she said warmly, flashing Giles a satisfied look. 'I must admit that I secretly hoped we'd be able to stay in this area. And for him to have Hill Cottage temporarily is marvellous.'

'I always believe that things have a knack of working out,' Paul told her.

'A very comfortable theory,' Giles put in, forcing a smile. 'But I must say I'm thoroughly enjoying being a kind of locum at the moment and getting back into the swim. My first experience of a country-cum-rural practice.'

Paul laughed. 'You'll sometimes stand in for Tessa! We're a pretty friendly bunch.'

Giles looked at Tessa as though his gaze had reached her heart.

'That will be a pleasure.'

Sister Allan came in, smiled at them, and said with an air of dismissal, 'Time's up, Doctors!' She looked at Rosemary with a warm smile. 'We want our patient to have an early night.'

Paul and Tessa said their goodbyes and went out into the corridor to await Giles, who was joining them at The Hollow for a late supper.

Rosemary queried, 'I shan't see you tomorrow, shall I? No visitors on operation days.' She added, 'Although—'

'You'll be drowsy, anyway . . . But I shall ring, and be in touch with Adrian.' Giles put his hand on her shoulder and then smoothed her hair with a concerned affectionate gesture, and didn't underestimate the trauma of what lay ahead. To marry her without being in love with her would be an insult; to break his engagement, as he must, would, he knew, shatter her. There was no easy solution; but the strain of the present relationship was nerve-racking and made him guilt-ridden. 'I shall think of you,' he whispered lamely, and bent his lips to hers in a swift light kiss. 'All over tomorrow.' His voice was reassuring and bright.

'You've been so patient—having me here like this,' she said appreciatively. 'Very dull for you, darling.'

'You could never be dull,' he commented genuinely.

Rosemary held on to his hand until he had reached the end of the bed. He joined Paul and Tessa in the corridor like a man who had escaped from an ordeal.

Randall had prepared a cold buffet meal and they

went straight into the dining room at The Hollow. Tessa knew that this situation would recur now that Giles was part of the pattern, and she must learn to be pleasant without involvement, making her attitude plain to him, while obscure to everyone else. Paul's happiness counted, and she knew that reservation on her part over Giles would mar his pleasure and satisfaction. There was a friendship between the two men which, even in that short space of time, manifested itself in an ease of manner, identity of views, and obvious harmony. When they spoke of the past they were immediately involved, forgetful of those around them. It was unthinkable that anything should jeopardise that bond. Her reflections were strengthened by Paul's observations about Giles' attitude to events when Rosemary was fit again. And while she had insisted that such an attitude was merely an example of his flirtatious irresponsibility, the judgment didn't apply where Paul was concerned.

'How about some white wine?' Paul suggested, as they gathered around the dining-table.

'I'd like that.' Tessa looked at the cold salmon and various salads, and realised that she hadn't eaten since breakfast.

'So would I,' Giles agreed.

'I've got a Puligny Montrachet.' Paul flashed Giles a wide smile. 'Our high days and holiday wine! Remember?'

Randall brought the wine and Paul opened and served it. He knew that Giles was tense, and sympathised because he was able to imagine how he would be feeling were Tessa having an operation the following day, no matter how simple. The word 'nothing', so loosely used, had little meaning when emotion was involved.

They helped themselves from the buffet and ended up

by sitting unceremoniously at the table as was so often the case, the atmosphere suddenly relaxed as they plunged into conversation that continued even as the light began to fade from the sky and the sunset fired the room, lighting up the windows. The Hollow was a sturdy Victorian house with large, high-ceilinged rooms, which had been in the Mason family for three generations. Paul had modernised it, replaced some hideous pieces of furniture while keeping a few antiques which he prized. It flanked Barton Street, but seemed to be divorced from its neighbours, by virtue of its solidity and design.

'Amazing how the pattern of life can change,' Paul observed with satisfaction. 'Time has very little meaning.'

'Yet a few minutes can alter the pattern for good,' Giles commented, his voice firm and prophetic.

'Or ill,' Tessa put in.

'I didn't mean it in that sense.'

'I know,' she persisted quietly. 'The cliché that we never know tomorrow is so frighteningly true.'

Paul said significantly, 'Knowing what one *wants*—' he looked at Tessa, a swift significant look, that made her lower his gaze—'is the important thing.'

Giles sipped his wine, adding, 'And being prepared to fight for it.'

Tessa forced a light laugh. 'On that note I think it's time I left you two to talk into the small hours—which I'm sure you will!' She got up as she spoke. 'Thank you for the delicious meal, Paul.'

'Thank Randall and Mrs Cross.'

Giles said unexpectedly, 'I think I'll get back to the Bell.'

Paul understood. 'Since Tessa's passing there—'

'Of course!' Tessa exclaimed.

'I shall be thankful when tomorrow is over,' said Giles sombrely, when he and Tessa were on their way.

Tessa felt quiet and sympathetic. 'Being a doctor on these occasions isn't the easiest thing. We can't relax into ignorance, and invariably swing between deepest gloom and euphoria. No question of ignorance being bliss; the possibilities always haunt us.' She flashed him an encouraging smile. 'Tomorrow at this time everything should be fine.' She might have been reassuring a patient.

'You and your father have been so helpful . . . You don't know how we appreciate it.'

The 'we' stung her, but she refused to allow it to shatter her mood.

'My father is a very special person,' she said naturally. 'A very human person; that's why he's much loved in the town.'

'As you are,' he added. 'I hear things.'

'It's a good partnership.' She felt a pang as they drew up outside the Bell. A strange feeling stole over her, part excitement, part apprehension. Tomorrow seemed a momentous day, and the obscurity of the reason emphasised its importance, since she was struggling in a vacuum.

When the car stopped, they sat suddenly very still; their awareness of each other overruling judgment, criticism, or any previous dissention.

'Can I ring tomorrow?' Giles asked quietly. 'Speak to your father?'

On impulse, Tessa said, 'Come to River Bank around lunchtime. My father should be back from The Meadows by then and you can have first-hand news.'

'And you?' The words seemed to slip out involuntarily.

'I may be there. That isn't important.'

He looked at her very levelly and might have said, 'It is to me.'

She didn't want passion to destroy her momentary calm, plunge her into any sharp denunciation, or introduce a personal note.

'Good night, Giles,' she said with finality.

He clicked back his seat-belt and opened the car door, looking at her for one lingering moment as he said, 'Good night, Tessa.'

She watched him walk into the hotel, and only her love for him had any meaning.

Giles arrived at River Bank at twelve-forty-five the following day. Mrs Wallace showed him into Tessa's consulting room.

'I'm afraid my father had to go out—a coronary,' she explained, 'but I know all the facts. Rosemary has obviously not come round yet, but her condition is perfectly satisfactory.' She indicated the patients' chair and sat down at her desk, indicating that she wished a professional element to dominate the procedure.

He relaxed slightly and said, 'Was it a vaginal myomectomy (an operation suitable for submucous and polypoid fibroids)?' His voice was enquiring and confident.

Tessa looked down at her blotting pad and then raised her gaze to his.

'I'm afraid not, Giles.' She paused and then added regretfully, 'It had to be a hysterectomy—complete. There was a mass of them, and the cervix had been infected.' She hastened, 'It won't help to evade the issue.'

'Hysterectomy!' he echoed.

Tessa never forgot the expression in his eyes; an expression of stark dismay, his cheeks paling as he muttered, 'My God!'

'I'm sorry,' she said. 'But there was no alternative. You know the condition as well as I do.'

He shook his head.

'We know,' he agreed, 'but we won't *see*. Neither Rosemary nor I, of course, discussed this possibility.'

Tessa could not fathom the depth of his obvious distress, and a sick hurt lay upon her heart as she watched him get up from his chair and pace the room. Obviously he must have wanted a family desperately, or this would not have been such a devastating blow.

'She'll be fine,' Tessa went on. 'Better than for a very long time. It's sad for such a young woman—' The words sounded trite and empty, and silence fell during which she did not take her eyes from Giles' distracted figure.

He tried to force a note of relief into his voice. 'Yes,' he said, 'she'll be fine. But that won't make the blow any less . . . Rosemary loves children.' His expression changed and became bewildered, as though he had parted from reality.

'And,' Tessa reminded him, pain stabbing, 'she'll need all your support. Your attitude will dictate the—'

'Don't you think I realise that?' he rapped out, almost losing control, as though Tessa were rubbing salt into the wound. Then, 'I'm sorry,' he added, 'I don't seem to be handling this very well.' In that moment he saw his future disintegrate; his hopes ruined, and the path ahead a nightmare.

'Shock is never easy to handle, and when coupled with concern for someone you love—' She faltered, then walked quickly to a cabinet from which she took a bottle of brandy and poured him a drink. 'Doctor's orders,' she said briskly.

'Tessa—' He looked at her with a dark brooding anguish.

'Yes?' She hardly breathed the word.

Giles gulped the drink.

'Nothing . . .' He held her gaze with a fixed, dazed intensity that was, in truth, a silent farewell. There would be no explanations; no past to recollect together; no future as he had envisaged it. And as he stood there, the fact that he was in love with her became a tragedy. He had known when their eyes met on that fateful night just over a week ago, and he had thought only of the moment when he would be free to tell her so.

Tessa sat down again, her emotions chaotic; yesterday and today inextricably mixed. She watched as Giles put the glass down with a gesture of finality, squared his shoulders and then said almost formally, 'Thank you for your understanding.'

'Won't you stay to lunch?' She added, 'My father should be back.'

'It's kind of you—but no. I'll see him later.'

Tessa hadn't any preconceived ideas as to how he might have taken this blow, but she realised that she had not imagined this total bereavement. In a matter of a few minutes he appeared to have become a different person, and the thought chased through her mind of how deeply he must care for Rosemary and counted on family life. And why not? Equally, why had his attitude to *her*, Tessa, held such passionate and sexual overtones? Everything he had said to her echoed mockingly as she got up from her chair and walked with him to the front door.

When he said goodbye, his words seemed prophetic.

He didn't look back as he walked down the short drive.

Letty appeared.

'Giles not staying to lunch?' she asked.

'No.'

Letty glanced at Tessa's face and decided that tact demanded silence. It struck her that Giles' advent had brought about a noticeable change in Tessa's moods.

Adrian drew up in his car at that moment and seemed to get out even as he braked.

'I'll tell Mrs Dewsbury to hurry lunch,' Letty murmured as she hurried away.

'Giles been?' asked Adrian as he and Tessa went into his room.

Tessa told him.

'Bad business,' he said, and sighed.

'Some men don't particularly *want* children,' Tessa commented tentatively.

Adrian raised his eyebrows. 'But all men like to have the privilege of decision. It's human nature to desire most the things we're denied.'

Tessa said fervently, 'How true that is . . . Will *you* tell her?'

'Of course.' He studied her. 'You're very involved with this case.'

'I—I like her.'

'Don't get too involved,' he warned.

She flushed and lowered her gaze. 'How is your coronary?'

'In intensive care. There's a chance. Been quite a morning . . . and you?'

'Routine—jabs for the holidaymakers, Karen needing antibiotics—chest flared up. Mrs Vale pregnant again —delighted. The fourth is only fifteen months!'

'Good to have some satisfied parents,' he commented.

'He's going to have a vasectomy when they have six . . . Happy family.'

'Brings a little light relief.'

Gradually they relaxed, the tension lessening. Tessa felt that her love for Giles was some tangible thing, discernible to others, and that her father's observant eye and understanding had already made him suspicious. She moved to the open window and glanced across to the river, which looked as though a myriad lights were dancing on its surface. The heat shimmered and only the faintest breeze stirred.

'What about your holiday?' Adrian asked abruptly and irrelevantly. 'Time you had one.'

'Holiday?' Tessa made the idea sound almost ridiculous. Then she added, 'It's you who need that . . . Letty deserves to get away.'

Adrian didn't protest: he looked thoughtful. 'Come to think of it, now that Paul has Giles in the practice and they could help out, a holiday is a distinct possibility. With Paul on his own, and overstretched—'

'I could manage,' Tessa protested.

'I don't doubt it, but I prefer you to have a back-up. And since you don't take kindly to our having a locum—'

'I've never made it an issue.'

'True.' He grinned. 'Neither has your enthusiasm overpowered me! Thank heaven Joan will be back from her holiday next week.'

Tessa mentioned the subject of holidays to Letty over lunch.

Letty looked delighted. 'I'd rather given up hope,' she admitted. 'If you ask me, you both could do with a Giles to help you out and give you more freedom.'

Adrian shot her a loving indulgent smile.

'That settles it. I'll have a talk with Mrs Wallace and get her to contact the agents. Where shall we go?'

Tessa could hear only the echo of her father's words, '*Now that Paul has Giles in the practice and they could help out—*'

'San Francisco,' Letty said promptly. She added with enthusiasm, 'I want to go on a cable car and see the Golden Gate. Everyone says it's a wonderful city, and they can't all be wrong!'

Adrian nodded, gave it a moment's thought, and said, 'Very well—done! We'll enjoy ourselves with dear Aunt Ellen's legacy.'

Letty gave a lovable grin. 'I had that in mind,' she admitted.

Tessa was delighted.

'But I must wait for the Latimer baby,' Adrian reminded Letty.

Letty held her breath. 'When's that due?'

'June/July—have to be mid-July. School holidays and patients away.'

'Which year?' she teased.

They laughed, but it was settled.

Meanwhile, the following day, Rosemary lay back against the pillows and faced a strange new world, looking through a screen of tears at the floral arrangement Giles had sent her early that morning. Adrian had talked to her—gently, encouragingly, and with deep understanding. Now she was thrown back on her own resources, courage and fortitude. There was no way she could brush aside what had happened, or minimise its magnitude and effect on life generally. The vital thing was to come to terms with it. Never to have children—hers and Giles'. And she knew, as she grappled with the fact, that she could endure the prospect for herself rather than for him. The agony of her suffering was on his account. What would his reactions be? There were, after all, very few men who did not want a son to carry on the name, or a daughter to spoil. The 'family' was an integral part of their life, and they were always so proud of the women who had borne those children. What had she to give him now? She swallowed hard; the physical discomfort increasing, the general weakness making her feel hot. How could she hold him to his promise? She looked down at her engagement ring and twisted it on her finger. Twenty-four hours ago it had been a symbol of hope; now it was like a reproach. The brave thing to do would be to give it back . . . A little groan escaped her: could any woman love a man enough to give him up? *For his own sake*. And was it for her to make such a judgment? Any minute now he would be coming in to see her, and she dreaded the ordeal. Would she be able to tell by the expression on his face the degree of his disappointment, even sorrow?

And in turn, as Giles approached the door of Rosemary's room he felt nervous and apprehensive, anxious only to make his sympathy and understanding a source of comfort. Deprived of the prop of professionalism, he felt stark and without support of any kind. The thought of Tessa stabbed with physical pain; the longing for her an ache with which he must now make friends. There could be no retreat; no escape. He hesitated for a second, took a deep breath and went into the room, knowing that whatever happened he must convince Rosemary of his love, even though his meaning was entirely different from her interpretation of the word. He could not desert her, or turn his back on the loyalty she had a right to expect.

Silently he put his arms around her, pressed her head

against him and held her as she whispered brokenly, 'I'm so sorry—so *sorry* . . . Oh, *Giles*—'

'There's only one thing that's important,' he said, holding her hands as he sat down beside her. 'You'll be better than you've ever been. This isn't the end, but the beginning.' He infused a note of brightness and confidence into his voice, touched and deeply moved by the sadness and fear in her eyes.

'We wanted children,' she sighed. 'This isn't fair to *you* . . . no, don't interrupt, please. Because we're engaged, it doesn't mean that you have to marry me now that this has happened. You're free, Giles. I couldn't bear it if it was a matter of duty, or—or you hadn't the courage to—to hurt me. Don't you *see*?'

'I see,' he said, his heart pounding, every nerve tingling as he struggled to make that final renunciation which would match her own unselfishness and, in addition, shut Tessa out of his life. 'I don't want to hear any more nonsense,' he hurried on. 'Nothing could ever change my feelings for you.'

'But,' she persisted, 'could a man continue to love a woman who can never give him children?' The words were torn from her in desperation.

Giles was thankful for the way she had phrased the question and, thinking of Tessa, said, his voice ringing with truth, 'A man in love with a woman would always put her before any children—there'd be no reservation. All this would merely be a shared disappointment.' As he spoke, and saw the overwhelming relief in Rosemary's tear-filled eyes, he knew that he could never have shattered her happiness when she needed him most, without losing all self-respect and peace of mind.

'Oh, *Giles*!' she whispered, happiness lighting up her pale face.

'Just one thing,' he added, 'I don't want you ever to talk like this again. The chapter is closed . . . Now tell me how you are.'

'I've been out of bed this morning for a little while, and Dr Lane has been in. I shan't be here more than ten days.'

He nodded. 'The time factor varies according to circumstances and individuals.' He was grateful to be discussing the medical aspect as he went on, 'We shall have to decide what's best when you leave here.'

'I shan't be *ill*,' she said, his attitude removing heartache and fear. 'It's discomfort, rather than pain . . . I've got a bikini scar,' she added with relief.

'You won't be able to lift things, stretch, or drive your car for a while,' he warned her. 'There's a great deal of healing to be done—but you know that.'

She sighed. 'Yes; I'm used to dealing with people who come back for check-ups . . . Oh, Giles; while one realised that it was a possibility, I never imagined that I'd need *this* operation.'

'We all bury our heads in the sand on these occasions,' he said with understanding, 'but you'll be better than you've been for a long while . . .'

'I'd hoped I could go back to the flat,' she said suddenly.

'Out of the question, unless you had someone there to do the work.'

'When do you move into Hill Cottage?' She looked at him tentatively.

'In about three weeks. I'm trying to get a daily. I can eat out . . .' He added, 'I haven't been *too* anxious, because you can always stay at the Bell.'

'It would be very lonely in a hotel.' Rosemary looked dismayed.

'I could stay on there. It's up to me when I go to the cottage.' He felt a little desperate. So much had happened in such a short space of time that he could not adjust either emotionally or practically. 'The moment you're fit again, we must find a place to buy and get my furniture out of store. I don't like this uncertain existence.' He patted her hand. 'Leave things to me. I ought not to have sold the London flat,' he added reflectively. 'But having decided never to return there—'

'And getting such an excellent price provided you could give vacant possession,' Rosemary summarised. 'To say nothing of your not knowing how long you'd be in Singapore.'

He nodded. 'You reassure me.' He smiled at her, grateful for her support. 'After all, we did agree that we wanted to settle in the Cotswolds,' he added, comforting himself.

'So, when it comes to it, things are working out.' She brightened. 'Your being with Paul—well! *That's* the most important thing.'

Giles was touched by her concern for him.

'And I wouldn't mind a hotel,' she told him.

His brows puckered. 'I'll have a word with Paul about it; see what we can arrange.'

Sister Allan came in at that moment. She felt sad about Miss Wynn; she was very young to have a hysterectomy, and wondered how Dr Rutherford was feeling about it all. Certainly the strained anxious look had gone from Miss Wynn's face.

Giles left a few minutes later, managing to accompany Sister and promising to come in again later, after surgery. He knew with satisfaction that Rosemary looked ten years younger than when he had entered the room.

'She'll be fine,' Sister Allan said brightly. 'A good patient.'

'Ah!' Giles said with feeling. 'It isn't the complaint, is it, Sister, but the attitude of the patient that counts?'

'That's very true. Miss Wynn looks very much better for seeing you.' They exchanged understanding glances. Around them patients walked up and down the wide airy corridor; nurses passed, their caps perched like little iced cakes on their bobbing heads. Giles relaxed into that world, grateful for its familiarity.

Sister Allan caught the eye of one of the staff who needed her, and hurried away.

Giles left and got into the car he had hired, prior to taking delivery of a new one. He wasn't aware of his surroundings until he found himself back at The Hollow, letting himself into the house and opening the door of the office where Miss Ross, Paul's secretary, and Judy Grant, the nurse-cum-receptionist worked, just off the reception area and surgery waiting room. Giles had learnt that Miss Ross was never referred to by her Christian name, and was one of the stalwarts devoted to Paul. Judy Grant, on the other hand, was in her early twenties, Miss Ross's junior by about twenty years, who was 'Judy' to everybody, and an outgoing modern whom Miss Ross liked while disapproving of her ideas.

Miss Ross asked with a certain tactful reticence, 'May we know how Miss Wynn is, Dr Rutherford?'

'Progressing normally,' Giles replied, not wishing to enlarge on the situation. 'Thank you.'

'Your patient's at three,' Judy told him, too brightly. 'A Mrs Fairly. Her notes are on your desk. She's only been here twice before, so you'll be seeing her from now on.'

Miss Ross, as old-fashioned as an antimacassar, rebuked, 'That's not for you to say.' Her parchment face creased into disapproval, but her eyes had been known to twinkle.

'That's all right,' Giles exclaimed easily, 'I'm going to be responsible for the latest patients on the list.'

'Paul's pets wouldn't like any change,' Judy quipped. She looked Giles up and down as she spoke, thinking that he could examine her any time, but adding, 'Understandable . . . coffee?'

'An idea. Thank you.'

'While you're here, Dr Rutherford,' Miss Ross asked formally, 'would you do this prescription? It's for Mycardol and quite essential. Dr Mason overlooked it.'

Giles said automatically, 'An adjunct to glyceryl trinitrate . . . angina?'

'Yes.'

He wrote out the prescription and handed it back to her, and she smiled at him over the top of her half-moon steel spectacles.

'Your handwriting must be a pleasure for the chemists. Most doctors' signatures are more like drawings than anything else!'

'And all the easier to forge, I understand.' Giles was grateful to be dragged back from his own tumultuous thoughts, and the immediate problems surrounding him.

'Really, Dr Rutherford?'

'I've been told that forgers turn the signature upside down and draw it . . .' Giles laughed. 'I'm not thinking of changing my job . . . thank you, Miss Ross.' With that he walked into his room, which had been hastily assembled, but which gave him identity.

Judy appeared with his coffee as he sat down at his desk.

'I'm so glad you've joined us, Dr Rutherford.' The words came impulsively.

'I'm glad to be here,' Giles admitted. 'You and Miss Ross are being most helpful.'

She smiled and walked jauntily from the room.

Giles sipped his coffee, staring into space, his world shattered as he faced up to the fact that now, the only reality in his life was work.

CHAPTER FIVE

THE problem of Rosemary's convalescence came up the following evening when Paul and Giles went to River Bank for supper after Giles left the nursing home. He had been accepted into the Lane circle as part of a team, and his love for Tessa coloured his relationship with Adrian and Letty, while the common ground of Adrian's profession discounted any strangeness.

'One realises the value of relatives at times like these.' Giles spoke ruefully as they settled down on the patio after their meal, brandy glass in hand. 'Rosemary hasn't any with whom she's kept in touch. And her few friends are mostly expatriates whom she sees on rare occasions. A hotel would seem to be the answer, but claustrophobic and lonely for a convalescence.'

Tessa watched him, aware of his presence with every nerve and pulse. Seeing him sitting there, apparently relaxed, emphasised a danger she had not foreseen. She could not keep up a cynical challenge, or even sink into the comfort of friendship.

There was a sympathetic silence.

Paul said, thinking aloud, 'It isn't as though she can drive her car at the moment. You could both come to me, but Randall—'

Letty interrupted, 'Rosemary would be more than welcome to stay here.'

Tessa felt she had been swirled from the first floor to the top of a twenty-storey building.

Giles said forcefully, 'But we couldn't possibly impose . . . you don't even *know* her . . .'

Letty retorted simply, 'She's your fiancée and you're Paul's friend. We've got plenty of space. Mrs Dewsbury and Ethel enjoy having guests, and I love spoiling people,' she added with an endearing grin. She looked at Adrian. 'Don't you agree with me, darling?'

'Most certainly,' he said honestly. Actually, if Letty had suggested housing a circus troupe it would have been all the same. 'There's a bedroom-cum-sitting room, and bathroom en suite, so she would be independent of us, if she wanted to be, and it would solve your problem.' He gave an encouraging laugh. 'Doctors don't want problems, and with your settling in to Paul's practice and all the anxieties of the past week or so—' His words were full of understanding.

And so the matter was settled. Giles' and Tessa's gaze met once and quickly fell away. Tessa realised that with Rosemary there, Giles would be a constant visitor. The prospect was shattering.

Letty explained about their forthcoming holiday, consoled by the knowledge that by then Rosemary would be well on her way to independence and emphasising that Tessa would be there.

Paul voiced his appreciation, thankful for the solution. He studied Tessa, aware of her somewhat distraught expression and relieved when she said, 'At least Rosemary will have a crop of doctors around her! I shall be happy to do anything I can.' She could not blame Letty for her generous gesture, typical of her nature.

The following morning, just before surgery, Paul said to Giles, 'The Lanes are a wonderful family.' The statemen begged agreement.

'Wonderful,' Giles agreed quietly. 'Their gesture is overwhelming.'

'Just like Letty. She'll be in her element.'

'You're very fortunate to have such good friends.'

Paul smiled, a little secret smile.

'I expect you've guessed.'

'Guessed?' echoed Giles, suddenly alert.

'I didn't intend saying anything,' Paul hastened to add, 'but in the circumstances . . . well—' he paused significantly, 'I've every hope that Tessa and I will be married before the end of the year.'

Giles stood there, shocked, speechless, before managing to murmur, 'I'm afraid I haven't been very observant, but . . . of *course*!' He might have been arguing with himself, knowing that he hadn't taken Paul into account of his own involvement with Tessa, his emotions so inflamed, his love so committed and his intentions so clear-cut, once he had broken his engagement. Now he understood Tessa's insistence that Giles' future plans had nothing to do with her. He had deluded himself about their renewed attraction. Was her attitude merely evidence of her sexual challenge?

Paul gave a little nervous laugh, knowing that he had been impulsive and precipitate in his confidence. 'That's just between us,' he said . . . 'Strange how our lives have suddenly telescoped.'

Giles felt that he was being bricked up by circumstances wholly beyond his control, and wanting to escape, exclaimed, 'Surgery—'

'Good lord,' muttered Paul, and looked at his watch. As Giles reached the door, he added, 'Have a meal with us tonight.'

'Us.' The word stung. Giles made an excuse, then began, 'I'm so glad for you both—'

Paul threw him a lifeline as he said a little selfconsciously, 'Tessa hasn't said yes yet! I just wanted you to be in the picture.'

Giles' heart felt it had lowered itself a few inches in his chest and then jerked back into its normal position. He was appalled by his own vulnerability, as he made his way to the practice quarters and faced Miss Ross in the corridor, dragged back into her precise organised world as he said, 'Now for the first patient.'

'There are five waiting already.' She looked waspish. 'Unless the appointment system is strictly adhered to—' Normally it was against her rule to indulge in the luxury of comment, but this morning her aged mother, with whom she lived, had driven her mad and she was desperate for a whipping-boy.

Giles was in no mood for opposition and cut in, 'It's eight-thirty-five, Miss Ross. I hardly think it will sabotage the whole day.'

She stared at him, mouth agape, as he strode into his room.

Judy, having overheard, chuckled, 'That'll teach you to tell him how to run the practice!'

'Run the *practice*!' spluttered Miss Ross. 'He's only been *here* five minutes!'

'But the patients like him! He's already "the nice new doctor"—news travels.'

'*Women!*' came a derisory grunt. 'Any attractive male—'

'Ah, so you admit he's attractive?' Judy was walking towards the reception area as she spoke, and threw Miss Ross a grin over her shoulder. Miss Ross dived into her office like a rabbit in its burrow, knowing that she had overstepped the mark.

Giles sat down at his desk and looked at the notes for

the scheduled cases. A new patient, Mrs Ellis, came into the room and he clicked back into a state of concentration.

Madge Ellis was thirty-four, a natural blonde with a fair skin and blue eyes, beautiful, but thin and anxious, as she sat down, nervous, ill at ease and faintly apprehensive because Giles was young and handsome.

He said with friendly concern, 'Now, Mrs Ellis, what's the trouble?'

She said with laudable directness, 'Burning gnawing pain below my ribs.'

He met her gaze with immediate response. 'Starting a couple of hours or so after meals, and continuing until you eat again?'

'Yes.'

Giles didn't hesitate as he said easily, 'We'd better have a look at you.' He indicated the adjoining examining cubicle which had been improvised until Giles' working quarters could finally be arranged.

She undressed and climbed on the couch. She was tense and apprehensive, so that as Giles began his examination he said gently, 'Relax . . .' His hands pressed just below the rib cage. 'M-m—it's very tender there . . . any worries?' he asked unexpectedly, his gaze direct but encouraging.

She hesitated, then, her eyes suspiciously bright, admitted, 'Domestic . . . emotional.'

Giles nodded, pulled the sheet up and said, 'Get dressed, then tell me about it.'

When Madge Ellis was back in the patients' chair, Giles said, 'You have a suspect duodenum. I'll arrange for you to go along to the hospital for a barium meal and an endoscope examination—' As she looked blank, he hastened, 'A device enabling them to see into your stomach. Nothing,' he added reassuringly.

'I—I *can't* start anything like that now, Doctor. I just *can't*!' She hurried on, 'You see—' Her voice broke and she shook her head, afraid that Giles would demand that she do as he suggested.

But he prompted, 'Tell me why not. Your problems. I'm here to help you, don't forget.'

Restraint vanished as she explained that she had been married for twelve years, had a daughter of ten, and that for the past five years had been in love with another man, and that they were lovers. Now his firm were sending him to Canada and neither he nor she could leave their respective families.

'We've known that his going was a possibility—he's in electronics—and dreaded it.' She sighed on a note of despair as she finished, 'We've been able to fulfil our obligations at home because we could *see* each other . . . My husband is a good person; I've nothing against him—nothing. But I can't love him . . . and I can't hurt him . . . It's the same with Max—my—my lover—and his wife. Now we're torn. It's like living with spikes in your heart.' She lowered her gaze. 'I'm sorry, that sounds . . . dramatic.'

Giles said with feeling, 'But like life, I'm afraid.'

She looked at him and relief showed itself in her eyes. 'Thank you for—for understanding. I realise you can't solve my problems . . . but just *talking*; *telling* someone.' She added on a note of anguish, 'Knowing what you have to do doesn't make it any easier to do—does it?'

Giles' voice was low. 'No; it doesn't make it easier.' His face was a mask. 'But indecision is the worst thing to live with. This conflict is a contributory factor in your physical condition . . . but you *must* be investigated, Mrs Ellis.'

'After Max has gone,' she stipulated.

'And that?'

She seemed to shrivel as she said, 'Next month . . .' She sighed in confusion. 'There are so few times that we can be together, I can't face waiting about at hospitals,' she went on. 'Please understand!'

Giles thought that he understood too well, and that the damage done by insisting that she carry out his orders might be greater than if he tried to alleviate the symptoms in the meantime.

'Very well. I'll give you a prescription for some Gelusils which will relieve the pain. I want you to drink plenty of milk and eat little and often—a bland diet. I shall make an appointment for you at the hospital next month.' His voice was sympathetic but firm. 'I don't like treating symptoms, and I want a promise that if the pain doesn't subside you'll come to me immediately.' He looked at her very levelly.

'I promise.'

'No smoking.'

'I don't smoke . . . I wondered if I had an ulcer,' she admitted.

'With diet and the antacid,' he said hopefully, 'we may avoid it.' He shook his head regretfully. 'I wish I could prescribe for your happiness, but tranquillisers and anti-depressants are not the answer.'

She agreed as she shook her head. 'I'd hate to resort to either.' She met his gaze. 'Thank you for being so kind, and for listening without making me feel . . . oh, I don't know—' her voice faltered.

Giles got to his feet. 'I want to see you again in ten days—assuming the condition doesn't worsen and you need me before then . . . And don't forget, if you want to discuss anything—I'm *here.*'

'That knowledge is like having a lifeline . . . I'm so grateful I've transferred from Dr Mylor. I could never talk to him.'

'We're both new to the practice,' said Giles with a smile. He paused for a second. 'You'll come through all this with courage.' There was confidence and assurance in his voice.

She didn't speak: she couldn't.

The door closed. Giles sat down at his desk again and for a second held his head in his hands; the thought of Tessa overwhelmed him. The possibility of her marrying Paul was the final blow—like a door being bolted and barred, instead of merely shut. His own words, 'This is not the end', turned a knife in his heart. He must have seemed so façile and, by comparison with Paul, little better than a philanderer.

Rosemary steeled herself to having the stitches out, only to find it was painless. The scar had a dragging sensation, and she felt that her stomach was distended, making her a little heavy and awkward. Otherwise she was progressing normally and feeling far better than when she was admitted. Her blood pressure was rising, and her pulse stronger; there was a sparkle in her eyes and an air of confidence in her manner. She had pleased the physiotherapist with the flexibility of her legs and general tone, and walked up and down stairs with determination, her objective being to return to an active life in record time. The news of convalescing at River Bank had brought tremendous relief, not only on her own account, but for Giles, who was thus spared the trauma of finding somewhere for her to stay. Letty had been to see her as an advance welcome, and Tessa had left her in no doubt of the hospitality that awaited her. In addition, Rosemary reflected, Giles was obviously happy to be working with Paul; also, Dr Warren had been more than willing to keep her job open, giving her the option of returning in her own time. He had secured temporary help, so that there were no worries on his account.

Settling in at River Bank was as simple as moving from one good hotel to a family home with an atmosphere of happiness, and the bonus of companionship. And while there was no question of any fuss, Letty insisted on her having breakfast in bed and all the little extra comforts conducive to her regaining her strength. Equally, Letty upheld all traditional orders, often accompanying Rosemary on her daily walks which began with very short distances and gradually increased. Stairs, to begin with, could not be taken without a certain strain and dragging awareness of scar tissue, but they were negotiated with a daily improvement, as Rosemary slid into the normality of everyday life, taking care not to stretch, or lift anything heavy, which would put a strain on the internal healing. Letty drove her out to the picturesque Hill villages and found tea-shops in unexpected places—black-and-white oak-beamed cottages, with old-fashioned gardens full of hollyhocks, pinks and large sunflowers growing in profusion.

'I've never felt so indulged—spoilt,' Rosemary said one afternoon when she and Letty were sipping their tea in a cool sixteenth-century house with a vast chimney corner, ancient carved chests and old prints adorning the panelled walls.

Letty had grown to love this gentle, appreciative girl, who in some ways was much younger than her years, and free from all pretence. She seemed to belong in the atmosphere of the past, and to uphold its traditions without any criticism of the present, or its unorthodox ways. The sun struck through the leaded windows and fell on her serene face, beautifying it. Yet Letty felt a pang. Giles' solicitude was noticeable without being mawkish, but there was a certain distraction about him that troubled her. She dared not face up to the fact that the same applied to Tessa.

And Tessa at that moment was facing Giles on the patio at River Bank. He had called to see Rosemary, having a short while between patients. Tessa also had a gap and was snatching a cup of tea. Mrs Dewsbury brought a cup for Giles, and extra sandwiches. She pandered to Tessa's love for the wafer-thin cucumber variety, and produced them miraculously whenever she suspected Tessa might have time to eat them.

'You're very lucky to be in practice with your father, and have the benefits of River Bank—plus your own cottage,' Giles said reflectively.

'I know; and I appreciate it. I could never take it for granted.' She looked at him with directness. 'I'm fortunate enough to love my parents.'

'Ah,' he responded. 'It doesn't always follow. We can't love to order.'

Tessa felt very still, as though a great silence had fallen, and Giles' statement was momentous. She had no desire to twist his words, or make them an issue. During the past weeks Rosemary's presence had wiped out an earlier antagonism; she treated Giles with friendly acceptance, avoiding argument or challenge and, by so doing, had built up a deceptive calm. But her emotions were as deep, as volatile and passionate as in the moments of their first meeting. And as Giles sat there, he said with the banality that concealed tension, 'You're all coming to dinner with me this evening.'

She nodded, 'You'll be back on familiar ground at the Bell . . . How do you like living at the cottage?'

'It's attractive; very comfortable, and Ethel's sister is looking after me very well. Arrives in time to get my breakfast . . . I like it; the views of Bredon Hill are magnificent.' He bit into a sandwich. 'Only a matter of minutes away from you.'

Their gaze met and held with mute enquiry. Each reflected that it might be a million miles.

'You'll be looking for a house to buy.' Tessa tried to keep her voice steady. 'I was warning Rosemary that it might take a little time. Property in this area is quickly snapped up.'

'It might be a good idea to get a flat,' He said, his voice subdued. 'No point in having a large house.' He added, 'Once Rosemary can drive again . . .'

Tessa nodded. 'She can look around.' The conversation was empty, a means of avoiding silence, rather than benefiting from communication. Neither, now, dared to indulge in more than the commonplace, yet Tessa knew that she was glad to have even these few minutes alone with him.

'Letty has been wonderful,' said Giles, enthusiasm injecting a note of eagerness into his voice. 'I've never known anyone so kind.'

Tessa smiled, a loving light of agreement in her eyes. 'It isn't difficult to be kind to Rosemary,' she said, and there was almost a note of warning in her voice. 'She's come through this magnificently. No trace of self-pity, and certainly no fuss about her present physical limitations. If all our patients were like her, life would be a picnic.' The words were torn from her almost aggressively. 'You're a very lucky man.' She stopped, shocked.

It was hardly the most tactful thing to say to a man deprived of the joys of a family, and she hurried on, 'Rosemary will make a wonderful wife, and you are her life.'

Giles finished his tea and got to his feet. His face was a mask.

'I don't need need to be reminded of that!' he exclaimed.

Tessa felt that a blow had been struck at her heart. From one tactless remark she had gone, quite unintentionally, to another, making her words seem an accusation.

'Giles,' she said in a breath, 'I—'

But he had gone.

When Paul arrived that evening, Tessa met him in the hall and manoeuvred him into her consulting room.

'I—I wanted to have a little talk,' she explained, 'before we join the others.'

'Trouble?' He was immediately alert.

'Not unless the thought of having me for your wife is that,' she managed to say, grateful for the opening.

His face lit up, his voice broke with delight. 'You mean—'

'Yes,' she said resolutely.

'Oh, *Tessa*!'

Tessa had made up her mind after her talk to Giles. At the moment she was wasting her life yearning for a man who had bewitched her, robbing her of common sense and plunging her into meaningless conflict. At this rate she would be lost to reason, endanger her career, and become a lovesick, spineless nonentity.

Paul's arms went around her and his kiss was gentle, as though he did not want to spoil the moment by a demanding possessiveness.

'I—I can't believe it,' he said as he drew back. A somewhat boyish expression spread over his face and his hand dived into his pocket and brought out a ring case. 'I saw this a month ago,' he explained, 'and tempted fate. It looked like you.' With that he took a half-circle of diamonds set in a thin band of platinum and slid it on her finger. 'It could be an eternity ring, too,' he added.

Tessa looked at the stones of fire as they flashed on her finger.

'It's beautiful,' she said, genuinely appreciative.

'We can tell them all tonight,' he said, his voice rising with delight.

She looked at him.

'Yes, we can tell them tonight,' she agreed, and struggled against the sudden panic within her. The ring gave substance to her promise and forced home the gravity of her decision. To marry Paul, whom she loved, but was not in love with. In *love*. Was being in love a sound basis for marriage? Was the heady, intoxicating and exciting emotion that surged over her at the sight of Giles a justification for lifelong commitment? Didn't the passion and desire of sensuality all too often bring wreckage? With Paul, she would have a harbour; her life purposeful, the bond of their profession giving them a mutual interest. A little bubble of happiness surged over her, vacillation at an end.

'I'd like to have a word with Adrian and Letty first,' Paul told her. 'Put them in the picture. I don't somehow like just announcing our engagement and—' he broke off. 'Must be an old-fashioned streak in me!' He looked at her for guidance.

Tessa agreed.

Adrian and Letty were delighted. They had never assumed anything where Tessa was concerned, or traced any pattern for her future, hoping only for her happiness. They could not fault Paul.

'You'll be able to keep her in order,' said Adrian with a laugh.

Letty welcomed Paul with genuine affection. On the surface it would seem to be an ideal partnership, but she wondered why there was an expression of near-sadness behind Tessa's smile.

Giles awaited them at the Bell at eight o'clock that evening. The hotel had been a travellers' haven for some three hundred years, and Mrs Craik wrote *John Halifax, Gentleman* while staying there, its timbered walls and low ceilings being much as they were in Elizabeth I's reign. To Giles it had become home, and the Lane family, as Tessa had previously told him, had enjoyed its excellent service for years. The owners were welcoming, the staff always helpful, but never obtrusive.

Rosemary, with a little gesture of happiness, moved to Giles' side, not having seen him since the previous evening. Her hand slid surreptitiously into his and then fell away, her eyes raised in a smile. She looked happy and glowing in a dress of cornflower-blue, soft and feminine. Tessa was aware of the gesture, but Paul's arm pressed against hers and she met his loving gaze. She looked like a sun goddess—striking in her favourite white, her hair shining, her skin smooth and a pale nut-brown.

'This,' said Giles, 'is a unique occasion! Four doctors let out!'

'We're on the spot,' Adrian put in. 'Mrs Dewhurst will get in touch if there should be any calls.'

'Randall, too,' Paul observed.

Tessa didn't want her gaze drawn to Giles, although his presence was magnetic. He looked impressive in his lightweight cream jacket and dark trousers, his casual elegance attracting swift looks of admiration. They went into the William and Mary Bar where, in winter, a large log fire burned. A Turkey-patterned carpet and red décor were bright against the white walls and dark beams. Rosemary looked around her with thankfulness that she was now able to go out, and not be apprehensive any more; and while she had not wholly recovered from the shock of realising she could not have any children, Giles' attitude enabled her to face the future with hope and fortitude.

'Look,' she said, as she sat down, indicating an ancient fresco work beneath which was written, '*Discovered in this room under 14 layers of wallpaper. This is the work of the monks during the 8th or 9th century, when this was the guest house of the monastery.*'

Giles looked with her. The others were familiar with it. 'Time,' he said, 'seems almost an illusion when you try to absorb such facts . . . now,' he hastened, 'drinks.' And for the first time he met Tessa's gaze with a consciousness and directness that made her body heat with an excitement nothing could suppress, saying in answer to his question a second later, 'Tio Pepe, please.' And all the time she was thinking of the ring on her finger, and of the moment when, as previously arranged, Paul should tell them of the engagement. He did so as they raised their glasses, his voice full of confidence and pride as he said, 'Tessa and I are going to be married!'

CHAPTER SIX

ROSEMARY'S voice rang out with naturalness and delight. 'How *wonderful!* Congratulations, Paul, and,' she looked at Tessa, 'every happiness.' She turned to Giles. 'Darling, isn't it wonderful?'

Giles felt that every nerve in his body had been frozen, and that the muscles in his throat were suddenly paralysed. But after a tense, almost electric pause he managed to say, 'I add my voice to Rosemary's. This is indeed a celebration.' He looked at Tessa and Paul in turn, his smile painted on his features. Nothing, he thought, that had ever been written about the torment of love could approximate the sick, hopeless sensation that made his heart feel like lead.

Tessa heard the sound of voices as though from a great distance, Rosemary's happily above the others, and was grateful when they eventually went into the Priory Restaurant, although she inevitably found herself seated on Giles' left at the spacious centre table, which he headed, Rosemary taking her place at the opposite end, with Letty on his right.

'I think,' said Giles, 'we'll part company with the niceties tonight, and put Paul next to his fiancée. I'm sure you can put up with Adrian next to you, Letty!'

'Any time, any place,' she retorted, smiling.

Tessa noticed the champagne in the ice-bucket—a Taittinger, which was her favourite.

'This is all delightful,' Rosemary said spontaneously, indicating the deep rose décor and white walls; the pleated fan-shaped napkins in a paler pink, and the glowing little red-bowled table-lamps on their short wrought-iron stems, adorning some of the smaller tables on which were pink tablecloths. Wall lights completed the picture.

Giles had selected a menu in advance, of lobster, roast duckling and a Grand Marnier soufflé, having recently carefully noted the preferences of his guests, and enlisted the help of the owners.

Watching him, Tessa was struck anew by his easy, authoritative charm, which made it unthinkable that anyone would fail to carry out his orders, while at all times conveying his appreciation. Emotion tore at her. She was sitting there, between Giles and Paul, her engagement ring flashing on her finger as the sun slanted in its direction—a circle of fire to remind her of her promise, and all that promise embraced.

The champagne took the edge off the conflict she sought to escape. Giles had a role to play as host; she felt desperately that she was playing a part as a fiancée. Paul's exuberance should have been a tonic, but it failed to lift her out of a terrible stillness which lay upon her like some intolerable weight. She was thankful that Adrian was magnificent on all festive occasions, his ready wit, wisdom and vitality making it seem impossible that he was of a different generation. Letty, too, carried the conversation with Giles. Paul and Rosemary appeared to be in a state of euphoria because they shared the common denominator of feeling secure in their love.

'We're a splendid crowd,' Paul said suddenly, 'when you come to think of it. I'm going to get about the best in-laws any man could have, too . . .' he grinned. 'I shall begin to sound smug!' He looked at Giles. 'I've even got the right partner in the practice . . . he might have been here for years!'

'I rather think this part of the world is my spiritual home,' said Giles, feeling Tessa's nearness a form of exquisite torture.

Rosemary flashed him a little indulgent smile as she said, 'Giles has a passion for the past.'

There was a sudden questioning silence.

Giles' voice was deep and low. 'Probably because I believe it's never lost.' He nerved himself to look at Tessa. 'What do you think?'

Tessa's pulse was racing as she replied a trifle abruptly, 'If you cling to the past, you lose the present.'

Paul beamed, 'My sentiments, too.'

Letty said brightly, 'I'm concentrating upon to-morrow and getting to Heathrow—praying that Mrs A. won't go into labour, or old Mrs B. won't fall and break her hip! I've lost a holiday before, and am definitely all for the present. I may have a soft spot for doctors, but they can't *guarantee* anything!'

Adrian looked from face to face. 'We're certainly well represented here tonight!'

'I think it's a wonderful profession,' Rosemary said appreciatively. 'And here, we're all involved with each other, too.'

Paul grasped at that to mention a matter that had been in his mind for days. 'That's certainly true. Adrian and Tessa look after you; I look after Letty—' he paused, 'it only needs for Giles to take care of Tessa, and the circle is complete.' He shot Giles a broad smile, then looked at Tessa. 'You couldn't possibly go outside the practice, darling! It would be sabotage.' He spoke with an easy confidence.

Adrian exclaimed stoutly, 'Splendid! I've been insisting that Tessa has her own doctor . . . she's evaded the issue by boasting that she's always well. Now she hasn't any excuse!'

Tessa sat there, trapped. To argue, to show any sign of refusal, would be to introduce an arbitrary note and rouse suspicion. *Giles*, her *doctor!* Nothing could be more ironic. She managed to say, flashing him an inscrutable smile, 'We don't seem to have any option, do we?'

Giles knew that there was no escape. To hint at an objection would seem an insult, and he told himself that the obligation would build a solid barrier between him and Tessa which would automatically impose a standard of conduct vital in his profession. He forced a note of lightness into his voice. 'No option at all. I shall be pleased to have you for my patient, Dr Tessa.' He was conscious that all eyes were upon him, and he flashed Tessa a quick look as he took a sip of champagne, to break the tension.

'I shall have to keep up my record,' smiled Tessa, 'and not trouble you.'

Rosemary beamed, and said generously and with significance, 'Later on, you may be glad to break it!'

Tessa felt suddenly hot and then cold. Rosemary's meaning was only too plain. When she, Tessa, and Paul had children . . . Emotion surged over her in a destructive wave. Her heart had no resting place, and she hated being so ill at ease. Even the perfect soufflé seemed difficult to eat, the muscles of her throat making swallowing an effort. Had she been mad to plunge into an engagement and thus add one folly to another? She took a deep breath. Cynicism struck its blow for sanity; her infatuation—she refused to call it love any more—would die and leave no more than an indulgent memory of stupidity. Reality lay with Paul, the future; a family. She drank a little more champagne and recovered her nerve.

When the evening came to an end and they returned to River Bank, Letty said, 'Thank you, Giles; it's been a splendid evening.'

Rosemary slipped her arm through Giles'. 'Isn't it wonderful to think that we shall be able to have many more outings like this? And that tonight is just the beginning!'

Giles nodded, dragging his gaze from where Paul and Tessa were standing across the hall, Paul's arm around her waist.

'They're an ideal couple,' Rosemary added, having followed that gaze. 'I'm so lucky to know you all. And it's so good of Tessa to stay here with me while you're away, Letty . . . Mrs Dewhurst and I—'

Letty interrupted her, 'I'll be happier this way.'

A few minutes later Tessa and Rosemary walked out into the drive as Giles and Paul were leaving, each in his own car. The night was full of the scent of wild flowers, and a soft breeze wafted from the tranquil river. The great canopy of the sky was a deep sapphire and a full moon lay golden and majestic, pouring its radiance upon delicate little clouds shading them to mother-of-pearl. No sound broke the silence until Paul said, 'A perfect night to end a perfect evening.' He kissed Tessa with naturalness, then turned to Rosemary, touching her cheek with affection. 'We all seem part of a family.'

Tessa stood tense, aware only of Giles, feeling that they must hear her heart thudding. And her memory of his kiss and his words, '*This is not the end*'. He looked down at her as though sharing that memory, then raised her hand and kissed it. 'Good night, Tessa,' he said quietly, turning immediately to Rosemary, who had moved a few paces away, wanting a minute with him alone.

Paul and Tessa walked slowly to Paul's car. 'I'll come over tomorrow evening,' he said, as his lips left hers in a farewell kiss. 'Funny to have you staying here.'

Their respective cars drove away. Rosemary waved. Tessa stood very still.

'Giles is really a shy person,' Rosemary said confidentially, 'although he doesn't appear to be.' She found it difficult to assess Giles' feelings for Tessa, and wished he could be a little more enthusiastic about her. It wasn't, she thought, anything he said, but rather his silence that prompted her apprehension. She hurried on, 'I'm so happy for you and Paul . . . he's a *dear*. I feel I've known him for years.'

Tessa's voice was warm and struck a truthful note as she said, 'Paul's a special person . . . I'm very lucky.'

They went back into the house and Tessa escaped to a room which had been hers since childhood and was still bright with old-fashioned chintz, bookshelves containing *Black Beauty* and volumes of the Brontës, and other favourite books which she kept there for sentimental reasons. The furniture was white, the bed brass; its frilled duvet and matching pillows in pink—the same shade as the carpet. A wide window-seat filled a circular bay and she curled up on it, like someone seeking sanctuary, as she gazed at the floodlit Norman tower of the Abbey in the near distance. It seemed the one enduring thing in her ever-changing existence. Her thoughts exploded suddenly . . . Giles, her *doctor*. It was strange, but the fact gave him a new dimension, increasing, rather than diminishing, his importance. If only she could hold one constructive thought for longer than a few minutes at a time; stabilise her motions, instead of allowing them to sway like a lamp in the wind. And on the heels of reflection she wondered why her feelings for Rosemary were so genuine and almost devoid of jealousy. Questions—never answers.

The telephone rang by her bed, and she picked up the receiver with resignation, always prepared for a call.

Paul said, 'I just wanted to say good night to my fiancée . . . am I disturbing you?'

'No; I've been sitting on the window-seat.'

'It's been a good evening, but we'll celebrate on our own when we can arrange it . . . you did rather spring it on me!'

She teased, 'Regretting it already?' Her spirits lifted. 'My ring is beautiful,' she hastened to add.

'How do I answer a question and comment on a statement at the same time?'

'I'm not thinking straight.'

He laughed, 'Then I'd better let you get some sleep!'

As Tessa replaced the receiver she made a vow never to let him down, and to be everything he had a right to expect. Only then could she justify marrying him.

She went through to the practice quarters the following morning feeling bleak and depressed. She both wanted her parents to go on holiday, and yet hated their being away. Once they had left, she would adjust; the last-minute preparations always brought trepidation. Everyone appeared to have made appointments to see Adrian, and treatment cards were either handed in, or they had tumbled through the letter-box in profusion.

'Why,' Adrian exclaimed, 'does my disappearing for

three weeks give patients the idea that I'm going to the moon?'

'Probably because, like doctors, they leave everything until the last minute!' she laughed.

'I'm a very organised person.' He shot her a challenging look.

'By the grace of your secretary, and your wife! They're responsible for your having this morning free to tie up any loose ends, and be able to leave for Heathrow at three-thirty! Thank heaven you've got a hire car to take you there . . . better sign those prescriptions, or you'll be in the doghouse . . . I've got a new patient to see from Dr Seabrook's list.'

'Pity he's retired; he's a good chap.'

Tessa nodded.

Adrian said abruptly, 'You won't stop practising when you marry?'

She looked outraged.

'That's the last thing! I didn't work hard to become a doctor only to give it up, I assure you!' She smiled broadly, 'Besides, you couldn't do without me!'

'The conceit of the woman . . . Paul may have other ideas.'

Tessa was emphatic. 'Paul knows me too well to voice them if he has!' She paused, then, 'You *are* pleased about us?'

'So long as you're happy . . . trite, but it's how I feel. I've always liked Paul, and he's tied you down so far as having Giles for your doctor! Your "I'm never ill" is too façile for me . . . But typical of the medical profession, who never obey the rules of the game!'

'And you've got faith in Giles?' Tessa hung on his answer.

'Yes.' There was a reservation in his attitude. 'But

there's something about him I can't quite fathom.'

'In what way?' Tessa waited, alert.

'Not my idea of a happy man, although he goes out of his way to give that impression.'

She chided, 'You're a romantic . . . he's just inscrutable.' Emotion flared. 'He's not easy to know.'

Adrian studied her. 'You don't sound exactly flattering.'

'I can't waste my time talking about Giles,' she said quickly, 'I've got work to do!'

Adrian stared after her, feeling that he was looking at a picture out of focus. He wondered why, since he had such a high opinion of Paul, he should have an indefinable uneasiness.

Paul hurried in just before Adrian and Letty left the house that afternoon.

'I'd love to have driven you to Heathrow,' he said, 'but—'

'Which is very good of you,' Adrian put in, 'but I like to go off without troubling people.' He gave a broad smile. 'We shall get to the Excelsior in time to have a quiet drink and a meal, and take off tomorrow morning without any fuss. The same applies to our return.'

'Very independent, my father,' Tessa announced.

'You take after him,' Paul said indulgently.

'Touché!'

Rosemary hovered in the background.

'Tessa will keep an eye on you,' Adrian said to her warningly, 'in case you forget the rules while we're away!'

'I'm reminded *of* those rules if I ever ignore them,' she said with a little laugh. 'I know my limitations!'

The car arrived; the cases were whisked away.

Letty, looking radiant and thankful that nothing had

happened to delay them, flashed Adrian a smile. 'So far so good!'

'You look like a honeymoon couple,' Tessa teased.

'We'll send you a postcard,' promised Adrian.

'Probably the day before you fly back!'

Paul stood beside Tessa with a proprietorial air as they watched the car drive away.

'The house already seems empty,' Tessa said, as they walked back into the sitting room . . . 'I promised to go to see Karen. This hot weather doesn't help her. We haven't seen much of the family recently,' she added, 'the time—'

'I've disrupted things,' Rosemary put in apologetically.

Tessa insisted that this was not so, merely that everyone tried to crowd too much into each day.

'I never realised,' said Rosemary, 'until I came to stay here, in a doctor's house, what medicine involved. The *tie* . . . the *telephone*!'

Tessa laughed. 'The summer's a picnic! You want to be here in the winter!' She tried to keep her voice steady. 'Are you expecting Giles this evening?'

Rosemary looked at Paul for information.

'He's on call, but he can transfer to this number, or the cottage, so no problem,' Paul assured her. 'What about you?' He addressed Tessa.

'Surgery. I want to be here this evening.'

'Then,' said Rosemary, 'I shall suggest that Giles and I go out—have an hour or two at the cottage . . . give you a little rest from us.'

She noticed Paul's expression of relief.

'What about food?' asked Tessa.

'I can cook something—I'd love that.'

Tessa felt a sudden unfamiliar stab of jealousy. There

was an intimacy about the prospective domestic scene that highlighted the situation.

'There may not be anything *to* cook,' she suggested unguardedly, 'Since Giles hardly ever eats there, apart from breakfast.' Even as she spoke she realised that she was presuming to talk for Giles.

'I've just thought of that . . . I can have a little walk to the shops and get something,' Rosemary said confidently, and seemed to become a person in her own right, rather than someone to be protected. She looked at Paul again. 'Is this a good time to ring Giles?'

'If it isn't, Miss Ross will soon tell you,' laughed Paul, then added seriously, 'I don't know how I managed before he joined me; he's taking over quite a few midders, and everyone likes him . . . must be off now, darling,' he said swiftly to Tessa, 'but I'll be back around six-thirty.' With that he dashed out to his car and was gone.

Rosemary said with startling unexpectedness, 'I've not really discussed the fact that I can't have children. With you, I mean.'

'But you can,' Tessa said gently, 'either with me as your doctor, or as a friend.'

'Do you think it's more important to be loved than to be a mother?' She added, 'If you had to make a choice.'

Tessa's heart quickened its beat. To equate being loved by Giles with motherhood seemed a simple choice.

'Some women are mothers first and wives second,' she said, speaking from her experience as a doctor. 'There are others with whom it's the reverse. I don't think you can possibly generalise.'

'Love can change,' said Rosemary. 'Marriages break

up . . . a mother's love doesn't alter.' She added, a little painfully, 'Love, to someone like me, becomes so *important*—the only consolation. Do you think it imposes too much on a man?'

Tessa found that she was trembling; that the wound of her own love for Giles was suddenly raw.

'Nothing is an imposition unless one accepts it as such. No man who loves a woman would ever love her less because she couldn't have children . . . That is your *real* question, isn't it?' Tessa's voice was full of understanding.

'Yes.' Rosemary's eyes filled with tears. 'You've said just what Giles said . . .'

Tessa sat there bereft, desolate; the words like a death warrant.

'Then don't think beyond that,' she advised, struggling to keep her voice steady.

'I sometimes feel guilty because I can almost *forget*. Then, when Paul talked about Giles and the midders, it all flooded back—the doubts and the fears, too.'

'Which is perfectly normal,' Tessa said reassuringly. 'You can't file emotions.'

'That's what frightens me,' came the cry, 'we just don't know ourselves when it really comes to it.'

Later, Tessa had cause to recall those words. But all she said was, 'We *have* to make friends with circumstances.'

'That sounds like a sad compromise, and certainly isn't applicable to you.' Rosemary felt it essential to establish the fact.

'We weren't talking about me,' Tessa corrected indulgently.

Rosemary brightened. 'I've got so *much*. Thank you for making me see sense. It's so easy to get things out of perspective . . . Giles doesn't like talking about emotion.' The words came involuntarily.

'Typically male,' Tessa exclaimed dismissively.

'Paul isn't like that,' Rosemary hurried on, adding hastily, 'Oh, I'm not criticising Giles, but discussion helps.'

Tessa wanted to read many things into those words, but resisted the folly. She looked at her watch. 'I must go to Avon House and be back for surgery . . . shall I drop you at the shops?'

Rosemary hesitated. 'I'd like that . . . could I have a minute to telephone Giles?'

Tessa nodded, and Rosemary picked up the receiver, getting through swiftly and coming straight to the point as she suggested a meal at the cottage.

Tessa walked to the door, but could not help overhearing.

'Go out?' Rosemary said. 'But it wouldn't be any trouble for me to cook . . . *no lifting* . . . We could have bacon and eggs! Oh, very well. You'll call for me about seven.' The receiver went back. There was a shadow of disappointment on her face. She had hoped that Giles would welcome the idea of being alone with her.

Tessa stopped at a chemist on her way back from visiting Karen and her parents, and having a cup of tea. To her surprise she saw Giles' tall figure coming towards her.

'Good heavens, what are you doing off the hook?' she managed to say lightly.

'What are *you*?' he countered, looking at her intently.

'Buying a lipstick.' She met his gaze, her emotions, resolutions, immediately chaotic.

He laughed. 'Not my line. I'm running out of soap. I

always thought that toiletries appeared in bathrooms of their own volition until now!' He added, 'I suppose there's no time for a cup of tea?'

The atmosphere between them was that of undiluted pleasure which neither sought to conceal. The warm summer day fostered the illusion that all was well with the world, and that it was enough to exchange a few words.

'I've just had one,' Tessa heard again Rosemary's words, 'Giles doesn't like talking about emotion.'

'And I really haven't the time,' he admitted, as they walked into the shop together.

It was a moment which created a certain intimacy and associated them in a domestic everyday fashion. Their arms brushed as they avoided other shoppers, the touch electric.

'You're taking Rosemary out tonight,' she said as though they were two people exchanging plans.

'Yes.' His voice was quiet. 'You'll be with Paul.'

'Yes.'

They stopped for a second, hesitant, reluctant to part.

'It's goodbye, then,' Giles said regretfully.

'Those words should be our theme song,' she said unguardedly. 'Lipsticks over here . . . soap straight on.' Customers pressed in on her as she moved away, feeling instinctively that he was watching her. When she left the counter, her purchase made, she walked quickly away without looking to see if he was still in the shop. He reappeared as she was about to get into her car, and opened the door for her.

'Since you're now my patient,' he said significantly, 'I must treat you with even greater respect!'

'I agree, Dr Rutherford.'

And as their eyes met, each realised that the danger of the situation was intensified.

Tessa managed the practice with skill and success during the following weeks, thriving on the added responsibility, the extra work, gratified by the confidence shown by Adrian's patients who had occasion to consult her. In addition she managed to spare time for Rosemary, appreciating that solitude could be a poor companion in the circumstances. Giles had been a constant visitor, Paul encouraging him and going out of his way to make Rosemary feel part of their association, and thus building up a personal friendship with her.

July slid into August, and it was a matter of five days before Adrian and Letty were due home that Mrs Wallace said as Tessa started morning surgery, 'You've got a new patient from London—' She indicated the case notes on Tessa's desk. 'A Mrs Carisbrook.'

'Ah.' Tessa looked down at the case notes which had been sent on. 'Neck; arthritis.'

'We could wring a few necks on occasion,' Mrs Wallace joked.

Tessa looked up and nodded. 'Now it's a question of ringing the bell and starting up.'

Mrs Wallace bustled out and Mrs Carisbrook came in. She was sixty, could have passed for fifty, and was wearing a smart cream cotton dress with a thin red stripe. Her dark hair was natural and her skin a fine texture with very little make-up. Her tall slim figure presented an attractive picture. She was obviously nervous.

Tessa welcomed her, put her at ease and said, 'I've read your notes from Dr O'Dell, but I'd like you to tell me about yourself.'

'Complaining about arthritis in one's neck seems—well, so trivial.' It was an apologetic opening.

'Nothing is trivial when you suffer from it,' Tessa said encouragingly.

'I *have* "learned to live with it", so the expression goes. Arthritis is invariably regarded as "nothing", and I understand that people don't want to hear about it.'

Tessa thought that it was a refreshing change to have ailments minimised instead of magnified.

'It's always easy to dismiss the other person's suffering,' Tessa exclaimed, feeling that there was a good deal more to be learnt about Mrs Carisbrook.

'How true.' Hands that had been tightly clenched in her lap relaxed; the humped-up shoulders lowered, and relief showed in the dark kindly eyes. 'The trouble is,' she hastened, 'that, recently, I've blacked out. It's only been for a matter of seconds, but I've fallen down.'

Tessa asked immediately, 'Any nausea or vomiting?'

'No; just literally falling down. A few bruises and a cut eye.'

'Are you giddy?'

'Sometimes; but it doesn't seem to be associated with the blackouts. And that word sounds almost an exaggeration because they're so brief.'

'You're giddy, too, when you look up, or change your posture?'

'Yes.'

'And the neck pain—would it, for instance, be worse if your head were raised on several pillows?'

'I couldn't *stand* that.' The answer came resolutely. 'I wore a collar about ten years ago; had traction and injections. Nothing really helped and I decided—'

'To learn to live with it,' Tessa prompted, quoting her.

'Yes; it's the falling down that . . . Oh, I don't *know*. Dr O'Dell didn't deal with this. It's only happened since we moved here two months ago. I've hoped it would stop.'

Tessa asked thoughtfully, 'Have you changed cars—your seating position in any way?'

'No; but I couldn't endure the head-rests that Nigel—my husband—had fitted to the car!'

'Ah! And your neck and *shoulder* . . . tell me more about the pain.'

'My left shoulder feels out of place.'

'So, in fact, the pain has got considerably worse lately?'

'Yes. Some days I can't turn my head to the left at all, and the back of my head aches. Everything seems to grate as though the bones are rubbing together.'

'Let's have a look at you,' said Tessa, her voice sympathetic.

Mrs Carisbrook could hardly bear her neck and left shoulder to be touched, and there was restricted movement in the spinal column. Tessa tested her heart, lungs, reflexes; made her walk a straight line, read the sight-testing card, then said, 'I shall want you to be X-rayed. When did you last have any done?'

'Six or seven years ago.'

'And I also want you to have an EEG.'

'What's that?' Apprehension crept into the question.

'An electroencephalogram—a record of the activities of the brain. Nothing to worry about. They'll attach electrodes to your scalp which are connected to a machine.' Tessa added swiftly, 'It amplifies the waves and produces them on tracing paper. It's painless and without any risk.'

Mrs Carisbrook looked suddenly agitated.

'It's my husband I'm thinking of in all this . . . you see, he's blind. It's been possible to deceive him about the blackouts. Once or twice he was out when I fell, and on another occasion I said I'd tripped over a rug. We laughed because he never stumbles. He knows about the arthritis and is wonderful.' She added, 'We've been married for forty years. He lost his sight during the war, and is ten years older than I am; we haven't any children. At seventy he said that life *began* then, and he's so vital—enjoys everything, refuses to accept his blindness as a handicap. If *I* were incapacitated . . . I mean, you can cope with pain, but not with falling down, because you can't keep it to yourself indefinitely . . . He would be wonderfully supportive, but—'

'I understand,' Tessa said gently.

'His uncle died and left us a house in Tewkesbury where we are now—and enough money for us to live in modest comfort. You'd hardly know Nigel was blind; he has enormous will-power and courage. He types; loves doing everything. We go to Stratford to the theatre —everywhere. The blind have a sixth sense, and I often think they see more than we do; they certainly appreciate things more.' A smile beautified her face. 'He's always planning surprises for me, and fresh places are a tonic to him. Married happiness doesn't seem very fashionable today, I know, but it's wonderful when you have it.'

Tessa nodded and said warmly, 'And heartening to hear about.'

'I just want him always to be able to live life to the full. It would be so ironical if I should be the one to spoil everything,' sighed her patient.

'We're not going to think along those lines,' Tessa

insisted. 'I can find nothing organically wrong with you, but when we get the result of the X-ray and EEG, we can decide what's to be done. Meanwhile, I'm going to try you with some tablets for the giddiness.' She added, 'Are you travel-sick?'

'Only sea-sick; but I can't close my eyes in a plane or a car.'

Tessa wrote out a prescription for Stugeron which was specially indicated for vestibular disorders.

'These are also good for motion sickness,' she smiled. 'So you can close your eyes . . . Just one other thing, have you noticed any particular room, or place, where the blackouts occur?'

'Yes,' came the immediate reply. 'The kitchen.'

'Ah! Bending over the sink, possibly looking up at shelves—posture again.' The facts tied in with Tessa's possible diagnosis.

It was the following evening, when Giles called to see Rosemary, that Tessa sought his opinion on the case, feeling slightly uneasy and wanting the guidance her father would normally have given.

'Paul says you're an instinctive diagnostician,' she explained, her attitude relaxed, the common ground of medicine divorcing them from emotion.

'That's very kind of him.'

Tessa listed the facts, finishing with, 'What would your judgment be?'

Giles didn't hesitate. 'Allowing for the disadvantage of not having seen the patient, I think you've got a typical picture of cervical spondylosis—pain and restricted movement of the neck and in the spinal column. Posture trouble. Turning the head, looking up, may well diminish, or cut out, the blood supply to the brain, causing a brief blackout. There's also the question as to which root lesion is affected.'

Tessa said honestly, 'I doubted my own assessment —I haven't had much experience with this type of thing. Giddiness is common enough. It's the *reasons*.'

'Ah,' Giles said with feeling. 'That's why it's fatal to treat symptoms.'

Tessa laughed, 'You sound just like Adrian!' But she felt a surge of gratitude. Support for a diagnosis was invaluable.

'And the prognosis?' she asked.

'Uncertain. The pain can improve, or even clear up, but—' he shook his head. 'I'd be inclined to try Stemetil or Stugeron for the giddiness, which may well prevent the blackouts.' He looked at her with directness. 'It's all very individualistic. What suits one patient and works wonders doesn't touch another.'

'I've given her Stugeron. She's played down the pain. She's a thoroughly pleasant patient—I *must* help her.'

'You will,' he said with confidence.

'Your best never seems enough, somehow.'

'Umm.' He sighed. 'True.'

Rosemary got to her feet. 'I'm going for a little walk in the garden,' she announced.

'I'm cold,' said Tessa. 'I'll get a cardigan and join you.'

'I put a warm dress on,' Rosemary boasted, smiling.

Giles got to his feet. Rosemary wandered ahead of him, knowing that both he and Tessa were still in their world of patients and ailments.

Giles had just reached the French windows when he heard Tessa's shrill cry and a chilling thump from the staircase. He hurried into the hall, only to see her body slumped against the bottom stair. She was inert, silent.

He reached her and supported her head on his shoulder, calling her name and then murmuring desperately, 'My *darling*!'

CHAPTER SEVEN

GILES' words, '*My darling!*', reached Tessa through the miasma of pain that racked her body. She was aware of his arms holding her expertly in case any bones were broken, and of the tenderness underlying his distress, the intensity of his emotion conveyed to her in desperate revelation.

Rosemary, having heard Tessa's cry, appeared from the garden, taking in the scene and gasping, 'What's happened?'

Tessa, partially recovering from the shock, lifted her head from Giles' shoulder.

'I fell downstairs,' she murmured, realising that it was her ribs and left ankle causing the pain. 'Let me see if I'm in one piece!'

Giles supported her as she managed to stand on one leg, unable to put any weight on her left foot.

'Ouch!' she said impatiently, 'the ankle's sprained.'

'It's swelling already,' Rosemary observed.

Tessa clung to Giles' arm.

'I'm quite all right,' she insisted, not wanting any fuss and finding Rosemary's fixed gaze a little unnerving.

'That's for me to decide,' said Giles with authority.

Rosemary cut in again. 'You're dealing with your doctor now,' she warned, looking from face to face.

Tessa shifted her weight from Giles to the bottom of the banisters, holding on to them while Giles got the wheelchair which was kept for emergencies, then took her into her consulting room and practically lifted her on to the examining couch. There he removed her shoe and, since she was not wearing tights, examined her foot.

'I think it's a torn ligament rather than a fracture, but we'll get it X-rayed tomorrow; *and* your ribs . . . meanwhile a cold compress and a bandage for this—' he indicated the ankle. Their gaze met and lingered for the first time in deliberate awareness, then fell away abruptly.

'I'm glad Paul's at a committee meeting and wasn't here—' Her voice trailed away. 'You'll find lint and bandages in the top drawer of the cabinet over there,' she said, trying to keep calm and not wince every time she breathed.

They didn't attempt to make conversation as he applied the cold compress and bandaged over it. Giles' movements were sure and gentle, and she tried to divorce herself from the fact that it was Giles looking after her; but the tension increased as he took her pulse, which was racing, respiration and blood pressure, carefully moving her limbs which had only surface bruising.

'I'm just a bit battered,' she said finally and with honesty. 'I can tell.'

'I shall be convinced when you've been X-rayed,' he commented. 'Meanwhile that ankle must be immobilised, of course.'

She didn't protest, but exclaimed, 'I've had a miraculous escape—been very lucky.'

He looked at her, his voice low as he said, 'Don't make a habit of it, Tessa.'

The silence that followed drew them together in absolute unity; there was a question in his eyes to which, involuntarily and helplessly, she gave an answer, the echo of his words tearing down the barriers and poising them on the edge of a precipice.

He moved swiftly away from the couch and swung the chair into position, saying in a matter-of-fact voice, 'Paul will be back from his hospital committee meeting any time now.'

'Yes.' She was trembling, not from shock, but emotion.

With professional cool and skill he manoeuvred her into the chair and wheeled her along the corridor. They didn't speak.

Paul had just arrived, Rosemary having greeted him with the news. He hurried forward, his expression fearful.

'No bones broken—just bruises and a sprain,' Tessa told him. 'You were right about my getting a doctor!' She was too aware of Giles and her own turbulent feelings to want to build up any drama. 'This chair is window-dressing. I shall manage with crutches tomorrow!'

'You might have broken your neck!' Paul exclaimed, horrified.

'But I didn't.'

Paul looked at Giles. 'X-rays?' he suggested.

'First thing in the morning; rest is the best thing at the moment.'

Paul nodded his approval and said doubtfully, 'I can't get away tomorrow morning, I've—'

Giles put in with an ease he was far from feeling, 'I'll take Tessa along.' He added, with a half-smile, 'They've accepted me at The Meadows.'

'Of course,' Paul agreed, but felt at a disadvantage.

Tessa said firmly, 'I've *got* to take surgery before I go anywhere tomorrow.' Instinctively she looked up at

Giles. 'The patients have a right to be seen.'

'I'll have a word with Matron and see if I can take you along before either of us begins surgery.' He spoke as though there was no argument.

Tessa ached all over; her head throbbed.

Giles went on as though sharing her pain, 'Paul and I can help you to bed—that's where you should be.'

She felt the frustration of being incapacitated. Pain didn't matter so long as she could be independent, but she admitted, 'I think bed might be a good idea.'

Paul shot Giles an apprehensive look. If Tessa was prepared to go to bed, *was* she all right?

Giles gave Paul a glance of reassurance he was far from feeling, not because of any fault of professional judgment, but because he was suffering the shock of her accident, his nerves taut.

'You don't fall downstairs, even if not sustaining any major injury, without getting a headache,' he exclaimed with a wry smile, and on a note that Tessa appreciated. 'An analgesic will help.'

Preferably Equagesic, Tessa thought, since that was for acute or chronic pain. Aloud, she said, 'I won't quarrel with that.' She glanced at Rosemary, who looked pale and distressed.

'I'm useless,' she said harshly.

Giles stared at her. 'Don't be foolish,' he said, surprised by her tone.

Tessa felt a strange unsettling anxiety.

'You can help me undress,' she said appealingly. 'I showered after surgery . . .' She looked at Paul. 'Now if you and Giles would get me upstairs—'

They almost carried her to the bed, Rosemary following.

Giles said formally, 'I'll go and ring The Meadows and look in on you a little later.'

Paul clasped her hand.

'I'll come back.' He shook his head. 'How I hate to see you like this!'

Rosemary said, as the door closed behind him, 'He's terribly upset, and so sympathetic.'

All Tessa could think of through the haze of pain was Giles' arm about her, the ecstasy that no suffering could diminish. She had chosen to come to bed in order to escape and avoid betraying the degree of pain she was acutely suffering.

'A good thing Giles was there,' Rosemary went on.

Panic gripped Tessa for a moment. Was it possible that Rosemary had heard Giles utter that endearment? She dismissed the idea, since Rosemary had not appeared in the house until after the incident; nevertheless she glanced up at Rosemary's face, which looked pale and rather set in its expression.

'Yes . . .' said Tessa, not really wanting to talk, but adding, 'Paul's a dear.'

'You make him sound like a pet,' Rosemary countered, and gave a little high-pitched giggle, which was unlike her.

'If I can wriggle out of this slip,' Tessa suggested, finding that any movement from the waist upwards was intensely painful. 'Thank goodness I don't wear many clothes.'

Even in those movements, Rosemary thought what a beautiful body Tessa had; its long smooth lines perfectly proportioned.

'I little thought, when I arrived here that first evening, I'd ever be helping *you* into a nightdress,' Rosemary remarked, the task over.

'No,' Tessa agreed. 'Life is one long mystery, full of surprises . . . If you could pile those pillows behind me—'

'One upon the other, like they do in—'

'Yes.' Tessa knew that lying down would almost be impossible. 'Thank you.' She gave Rosemary a warm smile, then, 'And could you make me a cup of tea? Mrs Dewhurst is out, as you know, and my mouth is so *dry*.'

'Sweet tea for shock,' said Rosemary.

'Yes; but tea without sugar for me, please,' Tessa suggested.

'That's a beautiful nightdress—the lace is so delicate, and I love that soft pink.' Rosemary was assessing Tessa carefully.

Again Tessa studied her with apprehension. There was something disjointed about the way she spoke, and she had not betrayed any particular sympathy.

'Giles will want to see you.' The words came abruptly.

'Ask Paul to come up,' said Tessa, ignoring the reference to Giles.

'Yes. I'll see about the tea.'

'Paul will bring it up . . . you and Giles can have five minutes' peace,' Tessa added hastily.

Rosemary nodded and went from the room.

Tessa relaxed into the luxury of not having to pretend. Her ankle throbbed and ached, and she tried to breathe without inflating her lungs more than was sufficient to survive. It was a matter, she told herself, of adjustment. The sudden silence and solitude were blessings. The thought of Giles possessed her, as she relived those moments in his arms. She did not even try to deceive herself. He *knew* that she had heard his words—the evidence was in the look they had exchanged when he was attending her. She could neither challenge, nor pretend indifference; truth had shone through that moment and nothing could ever be the same between them again.

Paul came in with tea and biscuits, putting the tray down on the bedside table.

'How now?' he asked, drawing up a chair and sitting down.

'Fine,' she lied. 'I thought coming to bed would be sensible and save a lot of trouble.'

He took her hand. 'And gives us this time alone . . . oh, not because Giles and Rosemary have ever intruded, but . . . well, it will be good when you're back at the cottage.'

Tessa made an ardent reply of, 'Oh, yes. It's so different here without Adrian and Letty.'

'Yes . . . you're feeling grim,' Paul sympathised.

'Bloody but unbowed! I'll be used to it in the morning.'

'You know better than that.'

'I may; but I shan't accept the fact.'

'I wish I could come to The Meadows with you.'

Tessa made an amused gesture. 'No need for anyone to come—'

'You can't drive—' Paul protested.

She had overlooked that fact, and made a grimace.

'There are plenty of taxi-hire people . . .'

'Thank God for Giles.' Paul added, 'I'm jealous of him.'

Tessa's heart seemed to miss a beat. 'Don't be—' She stopped.

'I was only joking,' Paul laughed naturally.

'The whole thing is a waste of time, anyway,' she exclaimed. 'I know how I am.' She looked at him speculatively. 'And if I've broken my ribs, there's nothing to be done, since we don't strap people up with Elastoplast or what have you any more. Whatever it is, it will heal.'

'You never know *what* damage may have been done,' said Paul. 'Giles is quite right.'

'You doctors always stick together!'

'And what, may I ask, are you?' he demanded.

'A patient.' She forced a smile.

'And a brave one,' he said admiringly.

Tessa had a last sip of tea and he took the cup, then sat quietly holding her hand, knowing that talking was a strain, and saying after a short while, 'I'm going to leave you now, then you can settle down after Giles has seen you. I'll telephone first thing.' He bent and kissed her with tender concern. 'Thank God it was no worse.'

A knock came at the door a few minutes after he left, and Giles entered the room, his presence inspiring confidence, his quiet manner reassuring.

'How are you feeling—apart from the pain?'

She didn't pretend. 'Shaken, but counting my blessings. I couldn't have been looking where I was going.'

'It doesn't bear thinking about,' he said hoarsely, and hurried on, 'I want you to take two Equagesic and try to sleep . . . if you'd like a sedative—'

'No,' she said hastily.

His dark compelling eyes were clouded with anxiety. They both knew that there was nothing he could say.

'I've arranged for you to have the X-rays early. I'll collect you at a quarter to eight.' He put the bottle of tablets on the bedside table. 'Water?'

She indicated the thermos jug.

And all the time emotion was mounting as he stood there, his concern for her deep; his desire to help uppermost, as the bleak feeling of denial overwhelmed them both.

He judged the distance from the bed to the adjoining bathroom.

'You must have crutches,' he said abruptly, dragging his gaze away from hers, 'in case you need to get up.'

Tessa was grateful for the thought. 'There are some in the cupboard by the front door—we keep them for any emergencies.'

'I wish there was someone—' He stopped awkwardly. Mrs Dewhurst and Rosemary were there. But *he* wasn't, shrieked the voice within him.

'What about people who live alone?' asked Tessa. 'I'm very lucky. I shan't have to cook—there are so many things when there's no one to turn to.'

Giles nodded his agreement.

'I'm going straight back to the cottage,' he explained a few seconds later, and paused before adding, 'If you should need me, ring, no matter what the time. I'm on call tonight.' His voice was quiet and professional.

'Thank you,' she said, aware of him and of the overwhelming need to stretch out her hand and take his; aware, too, that it was her doctor standing there, which, in some subtle way, added to the tension.

'I'll get Paul to bring the crutches,' he said formally. 'After that, take the pain-killers and settle down if you can . . . Good night.' He didn't utter her name, but in that moment they were both conscious of their surroundings, and the intimacy of the scene. The bedside lamp threw a little pool of light over the bed, leaving the rest of the room in shadow, while the tower of the Abbey was etched impressively in the near distance like a picture framed by the open windows.

Giles indicated the curtains. 'Shall I draw them?'

'Please.'

He pulled on the cord.

'Good night,' he murmured again, and the door closed behind him.

They made a fuss of Tessa at The Meadows, expediting the X-rays, which confirmed the fact that there was no damage to the lungs; neither was the ankle fractured. Only severe bruising and the sprain accounted for the pain which only time would ease. As Tessa was wheeled down the long corridors (Giles seeing a patient in Maternity), she thought that the last time she had been there with him was when visiting Rosemary. Sister Allan hailed her in the main hall, just as she was about to leave. 'I never thought the day would come when I'd see *you* in a wheelchair, Doctor!'

Tessa laughed. She was pale and pain-racked; she hadn't eaten anything since the previous lunchtime, and there was a hollow, faintly nauseated feeling in her stomach.

'I have my crutches, don't worry!'

'They're the last thing if you've got bruised ribs!'

'So I've already been told.'

'But you won't listen.'

'I don't belong to the stork family and unfortunately can't hop about on one leg!' Tessa added with a wry smile, 'Not even with a stick!'

'Doctors are the very worst patients,' Sister Allan said with indulgent severity. 'They never do as they're told, and break all the rules . . . anything I can get you?'

'Wings,' said Tessa comically.

Giles joined them. Tessa looked up at him and then quickly away, in case Sister Allan should intercept their gaze.

'Sprains,' she grumbled, as she and Giles were driving home, 'are a nuisance.'

'Torn ligaments connected with a joint, with all the swelling and bruising, can be damned painful . . . but thank God there are no complications.' He shot her a sideways glance. 'Paul and I have talked things over . . . his suggestion is that I should help you out—'

'You mean *work* with me?' She spoke in a tone of suppressed excitement.

'Yes; our surgery hours differ from yours up to a point, and I can do a shuttle service.' He paused. 'Have you any objection?'

'Objection?' Relief spread over her features. 'It would be such a help!'

'It was agreed with Adrian,' Giles added, 'that we'd be there in an emergency, and I can visit any urgent cases, once we've discussed them.' His voice was authoritative.

'I'll be thankful for your support,' she confessed a little weakly.

He swung the car into the short drive at River Bank and stopped the engine, turning to her. The silence was alive with the thoughts that were tearing through her mind as they sat there, suddenly still, emotion almost a tangible force between them.

Rosemary came out to the car.

'Everything all right?' she enquired.

'No bones broken.' Giles hurried around to Tessa's side and lifted her crutches from the back seat.

Tessa reached Rosemary's side. 'Giles is going to help me with the practice,' she said brightly.

Rosemary's eyebrows went up. '*Work* with you?' Her voice was rather strident.

Giles put in, 'Just for these few days, until Adrian gets back.'

'What a good idea,' said Rosemary, but her expression was bleak.

Tessa managed to get from the car to the hall, every thrust forward seeming to stab her ribs and make her head throb.

Mrs Dewhurst appeared with coffee as they stepped over the threshold, also asking anxiously, 'Is everything all right, Dr Tessa?'

'Perfectly!'

'Thanks be,' came the stout, relieved retort. 'I thought you'd be needing this.' She went ahead and put the tray down on the table in the sitting room.

'Now,' Giles said with authority, taking Tessa's crutches, 'lie on that sofa for a few minutes.'

Tessa did so gratefully, the exertion having sapped her strength.

Rosemary felt isolated. It was difficult to accept Giles in this new role with Tessa. She hated herself for the thought that in a matter of hours she herself had ceased to be in the limelight. Tactlessly, she plunged into personal matters as she asked, 'Will you be able to spare an hour this afternoon, darling—to see over that house in Bredon's Norton?'

'*House?*' he echoed, as though he had never heard of one.

'Darling,' she scolded, forcing a little laugh, 'we got particulars from the agents and arranged to view it.'

Giles felt guilty and contrite, but he explained, 'I can't possibly know what my arrangements will be today. Better ring and tell them—' The faint impatience in his voice suggested that she should have taken care of the matter herself.

Tessa protested, 'You mustn't change your plans . . . I—'

'You'll rest this afternoon,' Giles put in. 'That's an order. Now I'll see Mrs Wallace and bring you the appointment book, then you can tell me which patients you'd like me to see.' He might have been working in the practice for years as he strode along the corridor.

Mrs Wallace put down the receiver as he walked into her office. She had already spoken to Tessa on the telephone, so was in the picture, but only so far as the fall was concerned. She looked at Giles with surprise. She had met him, but did not know him. When he explained the situation and why he was there, she heaved a sigh of relief and smiled her welcome, handing him the day book, saying, 'The appointments are not heavy this morning . . . so many patients away in August, but there's Mrs Gregory, and she's more trouble than three normal people.'

'In what way?'

'Diagnoses her non-complaints, and is a first-grade neurotic who devotes her life to her health. She's transferred from two doctors in the area already. Dr Lane took pity on her. She'll love a new audience and will regale you with the ailments she had even in childhood. As she's nearly eighty—' Mrs Wallace laughed. 'The latest thing is her heart. Nothing less than angina!'

'I'm just in the mood to tackle her!'

'She drives her poor husband mad, and he's eighty-five! He *has* got a dicy heart, and is a dear.'

Giles nodded his understanding. 'The greatest affront would be to tell her she was well!'

'Absolutely *fatal*!'

'Don't put ideas in my head . . . and, Mrs Wallace?'

'Yes, Doctor?'

'Do all you can to manoeuvre the appointments so that Dr Tessa is spared as much as possible.'

'I will,' came the loyal reply. 'I'm so thankful you're here. I'll put the relevant cards on your desk for the patients to be seen now.'

'Splendid! I'll just go through this list with Dr Tessa and then we can start.'

Joan came in as Giles went out.

'Dishy, isn't he!' she said with a grin.

'Then you can take the case notes to him when he's ready,' Mrs Wallace said goodhumouredly.

Tessa looked in on Giles a little later, as he was engrossed in the notes, sitting at Adrian's desk.

'It's so thoughtful of you and Paul,' she said with a quiet gratitude.

'Selfish, really,' he admitted. 'What we wanted to do.'

It seemed natural that he should be there.

'I've spoken to Paul,' she said. 'He didn't mention this arrangement when he telephoned early this morning.'

Mrs Wallace came through on the inter-com. The first patient was being sent in.

They looked at each other, nodded, and when Tessa reached the door, she said, 'This is not what we envisaged.' The 'we' slipped out, identifying them.

Giles gave her a steady meaning gaze. In truth it was precisely what he had dreamed about.

Tessa managed surgery, her ankle raised on a stool concealed in the hollow of the desk between the drawers. The cases were routine, with Giles taking those needing examination.

'We never think of doctors having anything wrong with them!' her last patient, Deirdre Watson, exclaimed.

'Or of them having any problems,' Tessa added without thinking.

'No; not really.' The tone was reflective.

Tessa looked at the girl, about her own age, whose hair was like a purple hedgehog. She was wearing a shirt and bow-tie and had a round, rather impudent face, and an attractive personality. She wanted two months' supply of her contraceptive pill, Marvelon, because she and her boy-friend were going on holiday without knowing where.

'I can give you two consecutive months' supply,' Tessa said helpfully. 'Two prescriptions.'

'Nothing's simple, is it?' Deirdre Watson added, 'Not even the pill . . . I mean, one daily for twenty-one days, starting on the first day of your period, then seven days free . . . Daft. Why not something you can take all the time and have done with it? I forgot after that seven days the other month—it was hell.'

Tessa said helpfully, 'You could have an IUD.'

'But there's all the fuss of having it put in.' She gave a scornful sigh. 'We hop up there to the moon, but aren't very bright when it comes to everyday important things . . . I hope your ankle will soon be better,' she added as Tessa handed her the prescriptions.

'Trivial nuisance,' Tessa smiled. 'I hope you have a good holiday.'

'We shall; we may even stay in England. We don't know much about England.'

Tessa looked surprised. 'But you were born here.'

'Oh, yes; but we always go abroad for our holidays . . . might be a laugh to stay here.'

Tessa nodded. 'Anyway, don't forget to take the pill.'

'You must be joking! I've learned my lesson . . .

thank you, Doctor,' Deirdre hastened respectfully, as she got up from her chair and left. She liked Dr Tessa —nothing starchy about her!

Giles appeared the moment surgery was finished.

'Well?' he queried.

'Easy.' Tessa's heart quickened its beat as she looked at him. 'How did you get on?'

'Very well. Eulogies about you and Adrian. I stopped Mrs Gregory in her tracks by taking her blood pressure and telling her it was that of a young woman, and there was no reason why she shouldn't have the telegram from the Queen!'

Tessa gave a loud chuckle. 'When she's a hundred! You won't be popular.'

'Her heart's amazingly strong . . . I must get back to The Hollow, but I'll come in after lunch,' said Giles, glancing away from her, their awareness of each other acute, 'and do any necessary visits. Meanwhile I want you to rest. It's an order. Lie out in the sun this afternoon . . . and take the Equagesic.'

'Can't you possibly manage to go to see the house?' she queried with sudden anxiety.

His expression became completely inscrutable.

She said quickly, 'Only I'm going to telephone the patients—sort out the "can wait" ones.' She drew on every scrap of control. 'Houses are not easy to come by around here.'

He focused her desk without attempting to look at her as he said, 'I know that. We'll see.' He hurried to the door and then looked back.

'Thank you,' she said softly—and remained sitting there, staring into space.

Mrs Wallace brought in a sheaf of prescriptions. 'If you could do these—'

'Of course . . . Well, that's one surgery over,' Tessa added.

'Dr Rutherford is a charming man . . . doesn't seem like a stranger to the practice, either. Quite amazing.'

'That's because he's such an old friend of Paul's,' Tessa put in swiftly.

'I hadn't thought of that,' said Mrs Wallace, agreeing. 'You look very pale, Dr Tessa. Are you all right?'

'Yes; I'll have my pain-killers in a minute or two.' She made a wry face. 'I never realised how often we breathe, until I bashed my ribs; it will make me very sympathetic in future.'

'And a sprain's worse than a break,' Mrs Wallace said stoutly. 'You put a break in plaster!'

'Ah, but a sprain doesn't take so long.'

'When immobilised,' Mrs Wallace reminded her.

Tessa gave a little laugh. 'I'm not going to enter for the marathon!'

She signed the prescriptions and a few letters that followed, made the necessary telephone calls and returned to the sitting room where Rosemary was sitting reading a Frederick Forsyth novel. She put the book aside as she saw Tessa, and got to her feet, taking the crutches as Tessa eased herself on to the sofa.

Mrs Dewhurst brought more coffee and this time Tessa ate a biscuit.

'You must be starving,' said Rosemary.

'Empty,' Tessa agreed.

'How did surgery go? I saw Giles rush off.'

Did that mean he had not been in to say goodbye? Tessa didn't like to ask.

'I've been thinking,' Rosemary said, as she sipped her coffee. 'After Giles and I are married, I could help him and Paul out. I'm a fully qualified medical secretary and

I should miss working . . . I do now. And with Giles in the practice they may need extra help.' She looked at Tessa with a direct gaze. 'What do you think?'

'Sounds a good idea, although Miss Ross has been with Paul some time.'

'The practice is bound to enlarge with two doctors working in it,' Rosemary persisted.

Tessa thought Miss Ross would have apoplexy at the idea of a newcomer in her domain, and had fiercely resisted any additional help. Judy fitted into the scheme of things and was very versatile. The words, 'after Giles and I are married', stung.

'You could suggest it, anyway . . . I hope Giles can manage to see the house; I've narrowed the visits to two—'

'And I've got permission to view the house any time. It will be wonderful to get everything settled.' She added swiftly as though not wishing to be misunderstood, 'You've all been so wonderful to me, but I know you'll understand when I say how thankful I shall be when I can drive again, and get back to normal.'

'Oh,' Tessa replied with feeling, 'I *do*. It must have been so tedious.'

'That's just the word.' Rosemary held Tessa's gaze, 'Are you and Paul thinking of marrying soon?'

'We haven't really gone into it . . . When Adrian and Letty get back—' Tessa's voice trailed away. 'Everything seems—well, disjointed, without them.'

River Bank came to life the evening they returned, walking through the door as though not having been away. It had been a wonderful holiday, but returning was the most exciting part when it came to it.

'Well,' Letty exclaimed with a beaming smile as she settled down to her evening cocktail, 'but for Aunt

Ellen's legacy, we'd never have been able to afford it all; and although it's been wonderful, I'll be more than content to potter around Europe or Britain from now on. I don't want to see one more airport, or one more plane—not for a year, anyway! And if we can't leave without your nearly breaking your neck—!' She looked at Tessa indulgently, then at Paul and Giles in turn. 'Thank God you were around!'

Adrian added to that, 'And thank you for all you've done so far as the practice is concerned, too.'

Rosemary spoke up, 'Giles has loved every minute of it.' She gave a little nervous laugh. 'I'm coming to the conclusion that he's a workaholic!'

Letty looked startled. Rosemary's voice had an edge to it.

Ten days later, Adrian having given her a thorough check-up, Rosemary returned to her flat, and Tessa to her cottage.

Alone on that first evening with the house to themselves, Adrian said, 'Would I be imagining things, or was Rosemary different?'

'I think,' Letty answered discreetly, 'that we're all happy to get back to our normal routine. Rosemary must have found the time dragging.' She looked out to the darkening skies of September where dahlias heralded the coming of autumn. 'Now we can settle in,' she added.

'It's good to be on our own,' Adrian said softly, while aware of her evasion.

And as they talked, Tessa sat in the silence of the cottage, trying mentally to adjust to impossible circumstances, and to the seemingly insoluble and obscure problems.

The ringing of the doorbell startled her. She knew it

couldn't be Paul, because he was at a forensic science dinner in London.

But when she opened the door, Giles stood there.

CHAPTER EIGHT

TESSA looked at Giles and uttered his name, half in surprise, half in fear.

'I must talk to you,' he said, a note of near-desperation in his voice.

She led the way into the sitting room.

'Is something wrong?' The words came in a rush of anxiety.

'Nothing that hasn't been so since I first came back,' he answered solemnly, as they sat down opposite each other.

She didn't protest, or try to silence him; the emotion surging between them was too intense, too overwhelming to sustain evasion; and suspense hung in the air like another presence.

'We shan't protect anyone by pretending,' he went on as her eyes met his in mute appeal. 'I love you, Tessa; and I believe you love me.'

She said, 'You're going to marry Rosemary.' It was a statement of fact uttered without accusation.

'But you must know the whole story—that's why I'm here.'

'Oh, Giles,' Tessa said tremulously, 'doesn't it speak for itself?' She struggled to regain some of her former cynicism, to draw courage from an earlier distrust.

'No,' he answered fiercely. 'If Rosemary hadn't needed that operation, I should have broken my engagement the day after you and I met again . . . No, hear me out.' His voice was low and rang with truth, as he went over all the details of his relationship with Rosemary and how, even when he was in Singapore, he knew that he could not go through with the marriage. 'That's what you must believe,' he finished urgently. 'We can't go on floundering in misconceptions, imagining that our love for each other can be ignored. There's no strength to be gained from self-deception. It's vital to make you understand why my behaviour has seemed suspect. When I invited you to dinner that first evening, it was because I believed I should be free by then, and could tell you all about my engagement. I didn't want to go into the details beforehand. I was shattered when Rosemary arrived at River Bank and, overnight, my plans and my hopes were doomed.' He made a helpless gesture. 'And to have told you the truth then would have—' He paused and sighed, adding, 'It would have seemed so facile and a gross disloyalty.' His voice was masterful, 'For God's sake, Tessa, let's be honest: do you love me?'

Tessa knew she was defeated as she looked at him, his dark eyes challenging, his presence awakening every emotion and desire of which she was capable, until she whispered, 'Yes . . . I love you. I think I have from the moment we met.'

He sat there drawing on every ounce of self-control —her doctor, as well as the man in love with her, the dangers profound.

'Oh, *Tessa*!' he sighed, half-despairingly because of the circumstances. 'And you believe me?'

'Yes,' she said, without hesitation.

'And you heard me—when you fell?'

She nodded, a flush stealing into her cheeks.

There was a moment of deep silence before he said with agonising truth, 'I can't break off my engagement now, any more than I could before. The same rules apply. It wouldn't be merely a broken engagement, but a—a rejection. One more blow for her.'

'And I couldn't live with shadows,' Tessa told him, her voice strong. 'Rosemary is a special person; you're her life, and although she's tried to convince us that being denied children is something she can accept—' Tessa shook her head as she continued, 'that acceptance is measured by your love.'

The facts seemed to overwhelm him as he groaned, 'It's going to be such hell!'

They looked at each other appealingly, like two people hoping for a miracle.

'I ought not to have linked up with Paul,' Giles said irrelevantly, 'but I wanted to be near you—'

'Paul.' Tessa uttered his name with distress. 'How can I marry him and give him so little?'

Giles got up from his chair as though immobility tormented him.

'Sometimes we would prefer the "little" to nothing . . . thank God I came here tonight . . . being able to talk about things . . . Rosemary has found a house that she likes and I can't back out. Will the fact that you and I can see each other help, or be a torture?'

'Both,' Tessa replied weakly. 'But I'd rather see you.'

'Oh, darling . . . and can I possibly go on as your doctor?' he asked significantly.

'At least you would always be in the picture—as a right.'

'That's true.' He moved to the drinks tray and poured out two brandies. 'Strange; I'd find it easier to leave Rosemary if she were my wife. Then she would have some moral support—' He shook his head. 'I can't think straight any more, and yet anything is worth it to know that you understand and I have your love.'

'Nothing can take that away,' Tessa told him quietly.

He held her gaze and it seemed a caress.

Tessa felt again the magnetism of his presence; the appeal of his humility, with always that air of authority to add to his attraction.

'I shan't be able to come here . . . our lives will be lived in a goldfish bowl,' he warned her. 'Doctors are subjects for gossip, anyway.'

Tessa said with courage, 'We've made the decision; any false move on our part would endanger Rosemary's happiness and she would pay for it.' She spoke as though the possibility were unthinkable.

Giles looked at her, love and admiration in his eyes.

'Perhaps it will be easier when Rosemary and I are married . . . God, it will never be easier,' he groaned. 'You'll marry Paul?'

'Yes; I'll try to make him happy; to atone for not being in love with him.'

He burst out, 'Are we mad not to take our happiness—study ourselves and—?' He made a helpless gesture.

'And feel guilty whenever we think of Rosemary . . . have her ghost between us always. She needs you. *I* couldn't tell her about us; so how could *you*?'

'Oh, my darling; there's so much I want to say.' He spoke in an agony of hopelessness and then, swiftly finishing his brandy, their awareness of each other mounting; the silence of evening wrapping around them insidiously, sensuously, he exclaimed abruptly, 'I must go.'

They went out into the hall in silence, and there, suddenly, almost violently, his arms went around her and his lips met hers in a long passionate kiss that reawakened all the ecstasy of yesterday, as she clung to him in an aching need. Then, wrenching the door open, he left her shaken, breathless, and with a feeling of bereavement.

The long shadows of autumn fell over the land in the next few weeks and seemed to Tessa to reflect her mood, as she struggled to face a world of unreality where she and Giles were ghosts merging into the background of life—grey, unobtrusive, silent.

Paul said suddenly one evening when Tessa was having supper with him at The Hollow, 'It's time we fixed a date for the wedding, darling.'

'Spring?' she said, trying to control her voice.

He shook his head. 'Giles and Rosemary are getting married in April—you must know.'

Tessa said carelessly, 'I haven't seen them for over a week . . .'

'I didn't think she looked very well when I bumped into her in Cheltenham today.'

'In what way?' Tessa was immediately alert.

'Strained, pale. She was shopping in her lunch hour, we had a coffee, and she told me then. I assumed you knew.'

Tessa shook her head. 'She hasn't needed me professionally, and now the summer's over . . . If they're being married in April,' Tessa hastened, 'how about July for us?'

'Good time practice-wise, but a long way ahead,' he observed.

'With luck, we shall have fifty years to play with afterwards.'

'And great-grandchildren,' he said, watching her.

Tessa echoed his words, adding, 'It must be strange to be old. I often feel very old,' she added unguardedly.

'I must have a bad effect on you!' Paul studied her

intently. 'I sometimes wonder if that fall you had in August didn't shake you up more than you ever admitted.'

She laughed spontaneously. 'Good heavens, I've forgotten it!' She was appalled by the ease with which she lied. She would never forget; on the other hand, in the medical sense, she had told the truth. It struck her that Paul was dangerously perceptive. It also struck her that he looked weary, which was unusual for him.

'I think it might be a good idea if you got in touch with Rosemary,' he suggested. 'Ask her and Giles over to the cottage; then you can survey her with a professional eye . . . I know, we'll take them to Fairfield. It's time we went out to dinner. You check with Rosemary as to the date. Randall can have our number in case either of us is needed.' He went on disjointedly, 'I think Rosemary's been overdoing it recently.'

'Are you judging by what you've observed, or from what she's told you?'

'A bit of both. They've been unlucky with the houses, after all. The owners of the second one they liked decided at the last moment not to sell, apparently. Giles mentioned that he had a feeling it wouldn't go through.'

'Buying houses, and selling them, is a lottery,' Tessa managed to say lightly. 'You never know until the money is in your hands.'

'Or you've actually moved into the house. Thank heaven we haven't that problem . . . you like this house?'

'Very much.'

'Pity Chestnut Cottage isn't larger, so that Giles and Rosemary could have it.'

Tessa gave a wintry smile. That would have been the height of irony. Her thoughts were racing as she contemplated dinner with Giles and Rosemary. She had not been alone with Giles for more than a few minutes at a time since that fateful night at the cottage; they had avoided each other with a discretion that would have escaped the detection of Scotland Yard, trying to maintain a relationship befitting the circumstances, maintaining a loyalty and steadfastness which taxed their endurance to the limit.

'I'll get in touch with Rosemary,' Tessa promised when she and Paul parted that night.

Rosemary made no protest when Tessa said that it was time she had her blood pressure taken, and how about a visit to the cottage for lunch on Tessa's day off? They could catch up on the news as well.

Rosemary arrived, subdued behind the too-bright smile. She looked elegant in a wine-shaded cashmere suit, with a gold chain at the neck; she kissed Tessa warmly and said, 'I thought I only needed a check-up again in six months' time.'

'Ah,' said Tessa, 'that's Adrian's department. I just want to keep an eye on you, otherwise.'

'I've been very worried,' came the immediate comment. 'This house business has driven us mad. We're back where we started.' She added, 'But Giles will have told you about it.'

'I hardly see Giles now that you're in Cheltenham . . .' The remark sufficed.

'It has seemed a muddly time,' Rosemary remarked ruefully.

'Come and let me take your blood pressure.' Tessa switched to professionalism the moment Rosemary sat down in the patients' chair. Paul, Tessa thought, was quite right. Rosemary looked strained and pale. But it would appear that she had already given a reason for the condition, since worry took its toll on the nervous system.

Rosemary wound up her sleeve and Tessa put the cuff of the sphygmomanometer around the upper arm. The pressure was 165/100. The reading was far too high, particularly the diastolic of 100.

'Is it *only* the house that's worrying you?' Tessa asked, meeting Rosemary's gaze and struggling to forget that she stood between her and happiness; that she was going to be Giles' wife.

Rosemary lowered her gaze; her hands moved nervously in her lap. Then suddenly she raised her eyes and met Tessa's almost boldly. 'Giles is talking of our going to Singapore and marrying there. Not bothering with a house until later.'

'Singapore!' Tessa exclaimed, making it sound like the North Pole.

'Well,' Rosemary pointed out, 'his father and mother do live there, and his father is still a sick man.'

'Of course.' Tessa breathed deeply, but felt her heartbeats must be audible.

'He'd get a locum to help Paul while we were away,' Rosemary explained, looking at Tessa with an earnest expression. 'So you see, I—I haven't any peace of mind . . . I'd got everything *planned*. Things upset me.'

Tessa felt icy and sick. Once Giles got to Singapore, would he ever return to Tewkesbury? Paul, being Paul, would fall in with whatever he wished. Utter devastation faced her at the possibility of Giles being lost to her.

'I can understand,' she said quietly.

'I don't like spur-of-the-moment things,' Rosemary admitted. 'I like to see ahead; live in the same place . . . it was a wrench to leave Oxford—'

Tessa looked amazed. 'But you gave the impression that—'

Rosemary cut in, 'Impressions can be so wrong . . . we seldom see the true picture.' She added, 'The cliché that things are seldom what they seem is so true.' She made a little expressive gesture. 'There's all the conflict . . . I had to be honest with you, Tessa. You've been so good to me; looked after me in so many ways—'

'Does Giles know how you feel?' Tessa asked the question abruptly.

'No . . . I wouldn't spoil his plans. I'll adjust.'

A lump came into Tessa's throat.

'Ah,' she sighed, as she clutched at straws, 'but you've no reason to suppose that Giles intends permanently to live out of England?'

'No; that's just my fear . . . I love England. I know I'm seeing things out of proportion and being selfish.'

'Giles would never want you to do anything—' Tessa broke off and then hurried on, 'I mean, your wishes are so important to him.'

'I know, and I've always stressed that I would go anywhere . . .' Rosemary studied Tessa with an intent gaze, 'I don't seem to have the same confidence since the operation, and dread failing him. Here, with you all around me, I'm—' She hesitated and added, 'Safe.'

Tessa felt that her heart was being wounded. Every word Rosemary uttered emphasised her need for Giles and threw into relief the inevitability of her and Giles parting. How right her own words had been on that fateful night, *'I couldn't tell her about us; therefore how could you?'* Looking at Rosemary as she sat there, Tessa knew they would never rescind that decision, no matter how great their unhappiness.

'I want to meet Giles' parents,' Rosemary went on,

'but it isn't any good my pretending that they won't be disappointed over—over the grandchildren.' She looked at Tessa, hoping for reassurance and seeming to measure every word uttered.

Tessa's voice was full of confidence. 'They'll be too pleased to know that he's found such a wonderful wife to spoil things by dwelling on that phase. And you mustn't dwell on it, either,' she added with professional authority.

'I know; I'm being weak and foolish . . . If we'd been able to buy that first house . . . oh, I should have felt secure, somehow.'

'And you've worked yourself up,' Tessa put in.

'Yes,' came the forceful comment, 'that's absolutely right.'

'We must deal with it,' Tessa said firmly.

'Nervous tension . . . funny, even my legs feel all wobbly.'

'I'm going to put you on Aldomet to relieve the hypertension, but the great thing is to—'

'Stop worrying,' Rosemary interrupted.

'I'd be world-famous if I could prescribe a magic cure for that,' said Tessa.

'Meaning that *you* have worries?' Rosemary shot the question.

Tessa lowered her gaze and reached for the prescription pad.

'Doctors aren't noted for their tranquil existence,' she laughed.

'But you're settled—parents here, The Hollow ready for you and Paul to settle down in . . . Knowing you, and Adrian and Letty, has made me realise how much I've missed.' Rosemary stopped and drew in her breath rather pathetically. 'I'm being a misery,' she apologised, 'when the only vital thing in life is the man you love . . . forgive me, Tessa.' She made a little deprecating gesture. 'You're a very understanding person.'

'A doctor isn't very much good otherwise . . .' Tessa handed Rosemary the prescription, then said with forced brightness, 'Paul wants to take us all to dinner at Fairfield Manor. It's time we had a celebration . . . will you have a word with Giles?'

Rosemary showed enthusiasm.

'You can stay the night at River Bank,' Tessa went on. 'Letty will like that . . . Now let's go and have something to eat.' She looked at Rosemary very levelly. 'There are times when it helps to be a fatalist.'

'And to have you for a friend is the greatest help of all,' came the quiet comment.

Tessa felt a surge of emotion; of protectiveness, and a certain relief. Until then she had not wholly dismissed the fear that Rosemary might have heard Giles' words at the time of the fall. Now that ghost had been laid, and in some curious way, the bond had been strengthened. It was not until Rosemary had left and Tessa was alone that she dared to face up to the prospect of Giles' change of plans about the wedding and Singapore. She felt hurt, isolated; even ignored. Surely he could have put her in the picture? Turmoil and conflict mingled with distress. Had Rosemary talked to her within the confidentiality of the doctor-patient relationship, thus preventing the subject being mentioned?

Rosemary, however, brought the matter up as they gathered at The Hollow before setting off for Fairfield Manor, the following Saturday.

'I meant to ask you not to say anything about Singapore,' she said. 'Giles wants everything to be clear in his mind before he discusses it with Paul . . . I was talking to you in confidence the other day.'

Jealousy stabbed as Tessa said, 'I rather assumed that; but I'm glad you've warned me . . . How are you feeling?'

'The tablets have helped my head; it isn't so heavy and belongs to me again . . . Giles!' Rosemary exclaimed lovingly, as he came towards them in the hall. She greeted him with a kiss and slipped her arm through his.

Giles looked at Tessa, trying to be natural and succeeding only in appearing stiff as he said, 'A long while since we had an evening out together.'

'Not since the Bell—' Tessa began, and stopped.

'Your engagement celebration,' Rosemary put in quickly.

Paul appeared and Tessa was spared any comment. Giles' presence wiped out all awareness of her surroundings as they went to their respective cars—a precaution in case of emergency. For a second she caught his fleeting glance. Memories tore at her; emotion became a longing that reduced her to silence, her nerves taut, her body trembling.

A little later the four of them stood together at the entrance to the hotel. Tessa felt Giles' arm brush against hers as they looked out over grounds that lay bronze and gold beneath the radiance of the hunter's moon, a wall of beech trees, like a giant mural, etched against the sapphire sky. Paul and Rosemary, walking together, moved ahead of them.

Giles said swiftly, his voice low and urgent, 'There's something I must discuss with you.' He looked down at her intently as he added, 'When and where?'

CHAPTER NINE

TESSA heard Giles' question almost with shock, and made no protest as she tried to allow for appointments ahead. Her free time was spent with Paul.

'Next Thursday, after nine, at the cottage,' she suggested, tensing. Paul was spending the evening with his anaesthetist colleague, Tom Wright, and she was having supper at River Bank. It would be simple to leave early.

'Thursday, then,' he murmured as their gaze held for a second before they caught up with Paul and Rosemary and went into the hotel together, endeavouring to enter normal conversation.

The setting of spacious elegance provided an initial talking point as they sat down in the cocktail lounge, with its ruby velvet furnishings, deep armchairs and low oblong tables.

'This is a beautiful place,' Rosemary said appreciatively.

Giles added his praise.

'Tessa and I have wanted to bring you here . . . oh, for months,' Paul said warmly as they sipped the drinks brought to them, then studied the menu so that they could make their choice before going into the dining room. The restaurant manager welcomed them, Paul being a valued customer. He could recommend the grouse, he said in answer to Paul's enquiry. Rosemary wanted fish, and sole bonne femme was suggested, the final choice being grouse for the men and fish for the women, with Ogen melon to start with. The favourite Taittinger was selected when the wine waiter appeared.

Tessa tried to involve herself with what was being said, but, from choice, she would have preferred to remain silent. Giles' presence was both torment and ecstasy, and she realised the near-impossibility of sustaining a natural friendly attitude, when every word they addressed to each other seemed charged with emotion, prompting, on occasion, abruptness, or even argument. Terrified that Rosemary might intercept any exchange of glances, she avoided his gaze and resorted to looking around her, simulating interest, but without anything actually registering. When finally they went into dinner, she told herself that Paul had every right to expect her to contribute to the success of the evening and she turned to the topic of medicine as she said, her voice smooth, 'Oh, Giles—do you remember my mentioning a patient who had brief blackouts and suffered intense pain in her neck and shoulder?'

Giles hesitated for a second before replying, 'Come to think of it—yes, I do.'

'You diagnosed cervical spondylosis . . . you were right.' She wanted to go on from there but realised that she was in danger of becoming completely absorbed in the discussion as a means of escape, and broke off a trifle lamely, saying, 'I mustn't talk shop! I'm afraid I get very caught up with some patients.' Even as she spoke, she also realised that the remark was open to comment, since Giles was her doctor.

Rosemary said, 'You couldn't hope to be neutral with everyone. It wouldn't be human.'

'But,' said Paul with a wry smile, 'friends don't always come off best when they're one's patients.'

'Beware, Tessa!' Rosemary laughed. 'In fact we shall

both have to beware. As wives, we shall be even worse off. Some of the doctors I've known were absolutely blind when it came to their wives being ill. It can be an affront to mention ailments!'

Paul flashed Giles a meaning glance. 'We're not getting a very good future reference!'

There was a sudden abrupt silence. Tessa felt that the unreality lay upon them like some dark cloud, and prayed that only she and Giles noticed it. She drank the champagne, hoping that it might dull the ache that made her conscious of every heartbeat. She was aware of each gesture Rosemary made as she looked at, and spoke to, Giles, and no matter how she tried to infuse a note of happiness into her voice, the sound fell flat and empty. Dismay brought panic as she turned her attention to Paul, feeling that her smile was false and that he must be suspicious. She didn't want to think of next Thursday, or what it was that Giles had to discuss . . . After nine, at the cottage. Was she mad to have chosen such a time, and such a memory-filled place? Wouldn't some old inn, away from Bredon, have been wiser? She knew that it hadn't occurred to her; that her suggestion had been instinctive.

Rosemary said, 'Those were very absorbing thoughts, Tessa.'

Colour rushed to Tessa's cheeks; she jumped as though startled.

'One can dream in a place like this,' she managed to say, desperate to sound normal. 'I wonder if there's a ghost here?'

Paul studied her with gentle curiosity as he said quietly, 'Tessa has a habit of retreating into a private world.'

'Haven't we all a private world?' Tessa asked lightly.

'And a story to tell,' said Giles, his expression inscrutable.

'One which is seldom told,' Paul exclaimed unexpectedly.

Rosemary shivered. 'Suppose we drink our champagne and forget ghosts.'

'Quite right,' Tessa agreed, and brightened.

They finished their meal and sat over coffee, when a waiter bearing a telephone came to their table.

'A call for Dr Rutherford,' he said, and plugged the instrument in.

'Mr Young!' Giles exclaimed in surprise. 'Started . . . that's early . . . I'll come at once. And that will teach me not to agree to the birth being at home,' he said wryly, as he replaced the receiver.

'Mrs Young,' mused Paul. 'Her third . . .'

Giles had got to his feet and was looking down at Rosemary.

'We'll take care of her,' Paul told him.

'I've only got to go to Letty's!' Rosemary protested with a laugh.

'I'll ring you in the morning,' Giles promised. 'Very little chance of my joining you again tonight,' he added as he was walking away.

Paul grinned. Mrs Young was a patient whom he had transferred to Giles.

Silence fell. Paul asked for the bill.

'Thank you for bringing us here, Paul.' Rosemary spoke with genuine appreciation. 'Tessa was quite right; one *could* dream in a place like this.'

'I'll keep my feet firmly on the ground,' Paul commented. 'Someone must.'

'Are you psychic, Tessa?' Rosemary looked at Tessa intently.

'Mumbo-jumbo!' jeered Paul. 'Don't put ideas in her head!'

Tessa answered, 'If I am, I'm in a very unproductive phase at the moment!'

Paul shot her a look of puzzlement and enquiry, as he asked directly, 'Why?'

She gave a little nervous laugh.

'If you ask impossible questions, you can't expect rational answers,' she flashed at him with a smile, knowing that the attempt at banter had fallen flat.

Paul replaced his credit card in its case. Rosemary met his gaze with understanding. The evening had been rather like a beautiful symphony marred by faulty notes.

Tessa was grateful to throw herself into work during the following week and on the Thursday faced Adrian before surgery, struggling to keep her concentration intact.

'Sarah Rawlings has an appointment this evening,' she said.

Adrian recapped, commenting reflectively, 'Ah; she's living with Julian Westbury.' He gave a whimsical smile. 'Difficult to keep tracks these days.'

'They've been together six years.'

'Sarah just appears and disappears, doesn't she, and Julian's an artist? I don't understand his stuff myself, but I'm sure it's good by modern standards. I'm partial to the French Impressionists, but not a pile of bricks or a lavatory seat! I'm too involved with the latter, in our job, to enthuse over it!' He paused. 'You all right?'

'Perfectly.' Her gaze dropped away from his.

'You're losing weight,' he observed.

'Nonsense!'

'And snappier on occasion.' He stroked his chin and fixed his gaze on her face, surverying her with faint concern, aware of her resistance to any intrusion.

'I'd better begin work . . . see you later.'

Adrian sighed as the door closed behind her. It had become a habit these days, he thought, because she seemed like someone guarding a secret.

Sarah Rawlings was Tessa's last patient. She came in buoyantly, bronzed, and the antithesis of anyone who needed a doctor. Tessa greeted her warmly, and Sarah sat down in the patients' chair with ease and familiarity. She was thirty, with chestnut hair, and a look of youth that made her age a matter of conjecture. She had the firm slim lines associated with outdoor life, and said brightly, 'We've just come back from Kenya.'

Tessa was pleased with the word 'we', because it implied that Julian was still in the picture.

'I knew the tan didn't come out of a bottle,' she smiled.

'Julian's got an exhibition at the Hayward,' Sarah confided, then went on, 'I think I'm pregnant. I need confirmation.'

Tessa liked her directness and said, 'Then I'd better have a look at you and make sure.'

'I've missed two periods,' Sarah cut in. 'But I feel terrific—just one little faint turn, but no sickness. My breasts are tender, otherwise nothing to show for it.'

'You're lucky . . .'

Sarah had already gone towards the examining room, taking only a minute or so to undress and climb on the examining couch.

'There's very little doubt,' Tessa said as finally she removed her gloves and went to the basin to wash her hands. 'But we'll have a urine sample—' She turned, drying her hands as she spoke. 'You're pleased?'

'Delighted. It wasn't planned, but we've always been prepared for the eventuality.'

Tessa smiled broadly. 'We'll talk when you've dressed.'

Back at her desk, Tessa said, 'You're perfectly fit; in splendid condition.'

'We're not going to get married.' It was a blunt statement.

Tessa accepted the fact as she returned, 'That's entirely up to you.'

'To be honest, we're both scared,' Sarah admitted. 'Julian's had one failure and we've been so *happy* during these years.'

'The superstition that marriage would spoil it?' Tessa studied her intently.

'I think that "superstition" is the right word . . . our friends seem to be getting divorced at an alarming rate. We'd hate that. If a relationship is working, why spoil it?'

'It's a valid question.'

There was an earnestness in Sarah's voice as she said, 'Dear friends of ours had lived together for ten years . . . his wife wouldn't divorce him, and then she died and they were free. They married, and when I saw him last he said sadly, "Now I'm just a man with the shopping basket".' She shook her head. 'I couldn't face that.'

Tessa thought what gentle irony there was in life: she was sitting there, *her* happiness destroyed because she could not marry Giles; yet that was not altogether a fair analogy since she was not in a position to live with him, either.

'It's not unusual,' she admitted. 'I never quite know what it proves, since there are thousands of marriages that last for fifty years and more.'

'Meaning you think we're wrong?'

'Not at all.' Tessa was emphatic. 'When it comes to emotion we're all babes in arms. The more I see, in fact, the less I know. Here we get all the permutations. Each individual must make up his or her own mind. I believe all human relationships have to be worked at. There's no lottery ticket.'

Sarah was silent for a few seconds. 'Julian and I believe that, too. We're as much in love today as when we first met.' She hurried on, 'I'd like you to deliver me. At the moment we're staying with my parents, who've taken one of The Moretons furnished houses in Bredon. We like it here so much that we shall buy something in order to have a permanent home. I don't fancy being a nomad with a baby, just to conform to the public image of artists.'

Tessa had met Sarah's parents, Andrew and Martha, who had the charm of yesterday, but were as modern as today.

'How *are* your parents?' she asked.

'Fine. We're thoroughly enjoying being with them. They took the house for six months, but are staying on. Daddy retired early and had the idea of exploring England, having let the London flat for a year. At this rate they won't get much further than Bredon! But it couldn't be more convenient for us. Julian can pop up to London when necessary . . . you don't happen to know of a cottage for sale by any chance?'

The thought of Giles and the evening ahead distracted Tessa's attention, bringing a ray of hope tinged with fear. What was it he had to discuss? The possibility of it being Singapore was shattering.

'Cottage?' she repeated, aware of Sarah's gaze intently upon her. 'I'm afraid I don't . . . Now, let's get back to you. I'll want regular checks and I'd like you to attend an ante-natal clinic. We prefer patients to be delivered in hospital.'

'No,' Sarah interrupted adamantly and half-apologetically. 'I've set my heart on having our own home, and the baby being born there. *Please!*'

Tessa capitulated.

'Oh, and will you and Dr Mason come and have a drink with us? I meant to mention your engagement before. I hope you'll be very happy.'

'Thank you . . . yes, we'd love to come and have a drink.'

'Actually we're at The Moretons itself—near you.'

'Yes; I can see the house across the fields,' Tessa said with a smile.

'I'll ring you,' said Sarah, beaming. She patted her stomach. 'Julian will be thrilled!'

Tessa saw her out and went through to join Adrian and Letty. Adrian was subdued.

'We've lost Mrs Burgess,' he said.

'When?' Tessa's brows raised; her voice was shocked.

'Half an hour ago; I've just come back from the house. Cerebral. Her son and daughter were there for the evening. She was in her usual good spirits . . . seemed one of the indestructibles.' His expression was warm. 'Ninety—a good age!'

'We shall miss her . . . I'm glad she wasn't ill.'

Letty looked from face to face. 'And I'm glad I popped in to see her yesterday.'

Adrian poured out a sherry and gave it to Tessa. He and Letty raised their glasses. 'This is how she would like to have been remembered.'

They looked at each other and murmured her name.

Tessa left River Bank at a quarter to nine.

'Would you mind taking the calls for an hour or so?' she asked Adrian without giving the request undue importance.

'Not in the least.'

'Switch over when you go to bed.' She kissed his cheek. 'Good night, Daddy,' she said softly.

To Adrian, the use of the word 'Daddy' was more eloquent than words, and was like a silent cry for help.

Letty walked with her to the front door. While never asking questions, or prying into her movements, she and Adrian were nevertheless always aware of her state of mind.

''Night, darling,' Letty said normally. 'I'm going into Cheltenham tomorrow—anything you want?'

'A loaded question,' Tessa answered unguardedly, adding swiftly as she hurried out to the car, 'Haven't I got everything?'

Letty suppressed the instinctive reply, 'No'.

The cottage struck warm and welcoming as Tessa entered it, the central heating adjusting automatically to the chill of the autumn evening. She switched on two wall-lights and a desk lamp, so that the room was bathed in a golden glow which illuminated the surfaces of polished furniture, reflecting silver candlesticks and the cut-glass decanters on the gleaming drinks tray. Every sound was magnified in the deep silence, as Tessa put a comb through her silken hair and hurriedly changed into a lace-trimmed white blouse and slim black skirt, repairing her light make-up with swift accuracy. Then she sat down and looked at the grandfather clock which was as a few minutes past nine. After a short while she got up restlessly and went into the kitchen to make sure the coffee percolator was set, and the cups ready should they be needed. Her heart appeared to be hanging on a thread of suspense as the minutes ticked away like hours, her ears assaulted by the stillness which seemed to have a pulse of its own to emphasise the hush. Nine-twenty-five; even the telephone mocked her. He would surely ring if he were not coming. And then a car raced up the lane, braking sharply at the front door which Tessa opened. The outside light illuminated Giles' tall figure as he hurried towards her, and the faint smell of ether hung suddenly and significantly in the air.

'A patient went into labour and produced twins a couple of weeks early,' he explained apologetically. 'I didn't have an opportunity to ring you. I've just come from The Meadows.'

'That's the second early midder you've had recently,' she remarked, her thoughts swirling, as he came into the hall and they went into the sitting room.

He stood for a second like a man who had been running a race and had reached his destination, breathless, exhausted.

'I had visions of not getting here at all,' he said as he sat down, sighed, and squared his shoulders against the back of the chair.

They looked at each other with the same penetrating intensity as on that evening when he had first seen the cottage; words lost their meaning as emotion flooded between them, and only the awareness of being alone held them in the spell of their love for each other.

'Oh, *darling*!' he said hoarsely.

Tessa's eyes, dark, lustrous and passionate, were illuminated; her voice was shaken as she admitted, 'I'd almost given you up.'

The silence of apprehension fell between them. Restraint made him tense, his expression almost grim.

'I both wanted, and yet dreaded, to see you here,' he

said hoarsely. 'Now that I *am* here, I want to forget everything else.'

Tessa was trembling as she struggled to overcome the desire he awakened, and asked hurriedly, 'What is it you must discuss with me? I thought we'd settled things.'

Giles sighed deeply. 'So did I,' he admitted. 'But it isn't so simple. I can't live within sight and sound of you and behave as though we're in effect strangers, never being able to touch you—it's glorified hell,' he finished harshly. 'I find myself wanting to fight, to rebel against my own judgment. I'm afraid in the end I might endanger all we're trying to protest.'

'Oh, Giles,' she whispered, 'I know.' Her expression had a pitiful appeal.

'I couldn't settle anything until I'd talked it all over with you. I *have* mentioned the possibilities to Rosemary . . .' He didn't wait for Tessa's comment as he hurried on, 'I've got to get away, not just for my sake, but for both our sakes . . . My father is still a sick man—'

'Singapore,' Tessa said lifelessly.

'For a while, yes. I couldn't marry Rosemary here,' he added, 'with all the goodwill of friends, and your parents. Pretence is hard enough in any circumstances, but with the pressures of intimate associations building up around us . . . That dinner the other night . . . it wasn't anything one could define. All I know is that failure is breaking a promise to oneself, as much as to the other person. We've got to face up to ourselves as we *are*—our temperaments, weaknesses, strengths.' He leaned forward. 'We've had this time to adjust and live as we should have to live in the future . . . people exist without happiness, but without peace of mind, and with continual conflict . . . there's nothing ahead but destruction.'

Tears filled Tessa's eyes because she knew he was right, and that her strength was no greater than his, but that their deepest bond, and unshakable determination, was to protect Rosemary's future happiness. Only the method of doing so had changed, not because of circumstances, but the relentless revelations of time. They were two people who had arranged a dress rehearsal for a fine play, only to discover that the construction of the acts was fatally wrong. Tessa didn't want to accept what he said; she wanted to fight, to plead, even to beg him to reconsider his decision, believing that just so long as he and she could see each other, be together sometimes, it would atone for all that was denied. And then she asked herself, could they guarantee that they would be able to stop at just 'seeing' each other? That, no matter how good their intentions, they would not eventually be drawn into a deeper and disastrous relationship? The inexorable wearing down of will-power and the insidious build-up of desire and physical need, bringing eventual disaster, since he was professionally involved.

'I could go away,' she suggested. 'I've never promised that I would stay in the practice . . . but there's Paul to think of, too.'

'Do you imagine I've overlooked that aspect?' He shook his head.

'No,' she sighed, half-apologetically.

'It's unthinkable that you should leave Adrian. What possible reason could you give?'

Tessa replied with all the confidence that sprang from a sympathetic relationship, 'I shouldn't have to give any. Adrian and Letty are not deceived even now.'

Giles looked grave, then said quietly, 'I should want to go to see my parents at Christmas, anyway. Paul would appreciate that, and I'd make sure that the right locum took my place.'

'And you'll hasten the—the wedding?'

'Yes,' he said dully. 'Since I can't practise in Singapore, I shall have to take it from there. Something will be worked out. Just so long as you appreciate—' He made a despairing helpless gesture. 'Trying to do the right thing and cause the least upheaval isn't easy.' His voice deepened. 'Rosemary would prefer to be married here; she's come to regard you and River Bank almost as family and home. Leaving will cause her a certain distress, but set against the alternative—'

'I don't forget that.' The truth weighed down upon Tessa. 'Once you're married, it will be easier for you to make future plans and discuss them with Paul.'

'Yes,' he agreed with gloomy reflection.

'I seem to be in a vacuum where Paul is concerned,' Tessa said sadly, 'drifting towards the inevitable while trying to live up to all he has a right to expect from me.'

They sat there, each fighting to cling to sanity; to be matter-of-fact, the silence and the intimacy of their surroundings bringing an unbearable tension as Giles said earnestly, 'I couldn't endure disagreement between us so far as the plans are concerned. Your understanding is vital.'

Tessa looked at him with honesty. 'As you've explained it, painted the picture . . . oh, I *do* understand, but that doesn't mean I don't dread the future.' Her voice broke and words rushed out involuntarily. 'I couldn't come to your wedding . . . you're so right about all that. It would be impossible. We deceive ourselves in order to avoid the ultimate hurt.' She paused and added significantly, 'And I couldn't just be your patient, either.'

He looked down at her ankle.

'Dangerous memories,' he muttered. 'Just as everything around us—' He broke off and got to his feet in a gesture she remembered so well. 'And now,' he said with determination, 'I'm not leaving; I'm going to have this hour with you—steal it to treasure, knowing that nothing can take it away.'

She stood up and the next second was in his arms, their lips meeting in a deep penetrating kiss that sent a shiver of ecstasy over her. His body was hard against her own as he drew her suffocatingly closer, while desire stabbed and merged with the rapture. She clung to him in a wild upsurge of passion until he released her slightly and she met his gaze in half-questioning fear.

'I love you, my darling,' he whispered as they moved to the nearby sofa and lay together, emotion wiping out everything but its own need. His hand covered her breast as he cried, 'I've wanted you for so long—' It was a stifled cry of frustration, and his lips parted hers in a fierce demanding kiss that added urgency to their desperate sexual need, and made him pause while they looked at each other in mute, almost agonised appeal, the present and the future hanging in the balance. Then, almost roughly, he tore himself away, saying hoarsely, 'If I take you now, I shall never have the strength to leave you.' His eyes, dark, tormented, met hers with all the desperation of love and thwarted desire.

Tessa whispered, weakened and frightened by her own aching need, 'And I could ruin you.'

Drama crept into the heavy silence as danger filled the room like a vengeful ghost, and they knew there was no hope of fulfilment.

Giles poured out two brandies, his hands unsteady.

The tension seemed like another presence, mocking, challenging.

Tessa didn't speak as she took the glass. They might both have been in a state of shock. Giles returned to his original chair, knowing that, quite apart from professional consideration, he could not add the final disloyalty to his relationship with Rosemary. Her future as well as his own hung on the frail thread of his control.

After a few minutes, Tessa went and curled on the floor beside his chair, looking up into his face, her cheeks flushed, her eyes adoring behind the pain.

'No one can take these moments away from us—as you said,' she murmured, her arm curved across his knee. 'Oh, Giles, I love you so much!'

With a convulsive movement he bent and kissed her lips, almost bruising them, then, gently and with resolve, kissed her forehead before saying hoarsely, 'Now go back where I can see you, but not touch you.'

She returned to her chair, her heart thudding so heavily that she felt it must be audible. They knew there were no more words to be said, and that he must leave her.

'Oh, Tessa,' he murmured, as after a few seconds he got to his feet.

She stood silent, numbed, wanting to cry out for him not to go.

'Don't come to the door,' he told her, his voice commanding. 'Always know that I love you.'

His car raced away in the empty silence. Tessa remained standing, great sobs choking her, tears running down her face. Everything in her word seemed to die in that moment.

CHAPTER TEN

THE telephone rang on Paul's private line and Rosemary asked, 'Are you alone?'

'Yes,' he said, surprised and immediately alert.

'Can you come to see me? It's important, Paul.' She was brief but resolute. 'I have the day off, so any time.'

'About two,' he suggested without questioning her.

'I'll explain then.'

Paul was punctual. He had been to the flat near the Promenade once or twice with Giles and Tessa, and managed to park outside the Georgian building, shivering in the grey dampness of the November day as he got out of his car. A strange sensation of near-doom assailed him as he rang the front door-bell. Rosemary would not send for him on any flimsy pretext.

She greeted him, looking pale, but composed; saying as they went into the sitting room and sat down, 'I'm sorry to have seemed so mysterious, but I couldn't talk over the telephone, and I knew you'd be busy, anyway.'

'Trouble?' His gaze didn't leave her face and the remark begged a denial.

She lowered her gaze for a second, then raised it to meet his.

'Facing up to reality,' she said.

'Ah!' He felt frozen into a state of trepidation, capable only of exclamations.

'It won't help, to avoid the issue,' she went on, amazed by her own calm. 'I'm going to break my engagement to Giles, but I don't know how to go about it.'

The sudden silence was electric and Paul shattered it like thunder as he said heavily, 'Because you know that he and Tessa are in love?'

She gave a little cry as all pretence fell away.

'Oh, Paul,' she whispered, 'I'm so sorry. I wondered if you'd guessed.' She hurried on, 'You're the only person I can turn to—the only friend I have, and I need your guidance.' Her gaze met his. 'Somehow I feel we understand each other.'

'I feel that, too,' Paul admitted, adding ruefully, 'I haven't known how to deal with my situation, either . . . what made you realise?'

Rosemary could not bring herself to tell him that she had heard Giles the night of the fall, and that his words, '*My darling*', had remained like a dagger in her heart ever since. Now she sat there, accepting what she had always known: that Giles' love for her had never matched her own. His kisses were those of a friend, not a lover. He had avoided being alone with her, and while she had insisted that things would alter when they were married, she knew it was a forlorn hope. To have discussed it all would have been to precipitate a crisis, and that was the last thing she had wanted. She believed him when he had insisted, after the operation, that to a man in love, the fact that she couldn't have children would not make any difference; but she knew, also, that he was talking in the abstract, and as a man bound by honour.

'I sensed it at the time of Tessa's fall,' she said truthfully, 'and suspicion has become a certainty since then.' She added fearlessly, 'I'm sure that had I not needed the operation, Giles would have broken our engagement when he returned from Singapore.'

Paul asked, 'How can you be sure?'

'Instinct—intuition. But if I broke my engagement to

him, it would have to be something very dramatic for Giles to believe that I'd ceased to love him,' she went on honestly. 'He'd think I was making a sacrifice, and never convince himself that he hadn't failed me. And if I told him I knew he loved Tessa, the result would be the same. You can't look at me and say I'm wrong, Paul, can you?'

Paul's sigh was deep. 'No,' he admitted.

She added boldly, 'Tessa could easily break her engagement to *you*, but the trouble is that she loves you as Giles loves me—'

Paul challenged, protestingly, 'What are you talking about?'

'The truth. They love us, but are not *in love* with us. And since Tessa can't marry Giles, there's no one else with whom she would rather spend her life.'

There was a depth of understanding in Paul's voice as he said quietly, 'That sums it up; it sums it up perfectly. You're a very wonderful girl.'

In that moment Paul took the dark secret from its shadows, and faced up to the fact that he had always known: that Tessa had not loved him as he loved her. He had told himself that he was content and that, with marriage, would come a deeper, more passionate bond. It was Giles who had held up the mirror forcing him to see the reflection of his own desires. The tension, the depth of feeling engendered when Giles and Tessa had even been in the same room together, tormented him.

Rosemary said desperately, 'I want to find a way out, Paul—to match their sacrifice. They're giving up love when they could find happiness . . . What can we *do*?'

'God knows,' he said desperately. Then, 'Aren't we building this up—dramatising it?'

They looked at each other, trying to find an escape from their own hurt. But Rosemary said wistfully, 'You know we're not. That's why I asked you to come here. I'm not capable of fighting alone any more. I know that sounds weak, but I've lived with the problem and how to solve it—' She paused, her voice breaking, her eyes filling with tears.

'Until you've made yourself ill,' he said gently, and clutched at the last thread of hope as he hurried on. 'But couldn't things change when you get to Singapore and marry? Giles has put all his affairs in order here and I've agreed to a locum who starts next week.'

Rosemary made a pathetic gesture. 'All those arrangements have been made out of loyalty to me,' she insisted. 'He couldn't face marriage here, with Tessa a guest. I can see it all. Oh, he would visit his father in any case, but don't let's deceive ourselves; the rest is—is wreckage for him and for her.'

Paul leaned back limply in his chair. He knew she was right and admitted, 'Self-deception can be the worst folly of all.'

'We're supposed to be leaving here in three weeks,' Rosemary reminded him. 'Christmas fills me with dread. Everything, now, is a charade—like that dinner at Fairfield. We avoid going to River Bank, and Giles is so kind, so thoughtful.'

'God,' Paul exclaimed, 'I know all about that! Tessa would agree to anything I suggested, no matter how outrageous. And Giles has taken on far too much of the work-load. I've seen him looking positively grey. The worst part is that we're friends; I can't release any of the tension by hating him.'

Rosemary's expression was full of sympathy.

'I feel just the same about Tessa . . . Oh, Paul; what can we do?' She looked at him with trusting appeal. 'I can't marry Giles; neither can I leave him with the feeling that he's let me down.'

'There must be a way out, a solution . . . There *has* to be,' said Paul, almost fiercely.

'I'm so thankful I've talked to you; that we understand each other,' she said fervently.

'Leave it to me to think of something . . . trust me, Rosemary.' He leaned forward and took her hand. 'I may find a new angle to all this.'

'I pray you do,' she whispered. 'I'll agree to anything you say. You're wise and—and fair.'

'Fair, I hope; wise . . .' he gave a wintry smile, 'perhaps wisdom will come.'

Rosemary reminded him urgently, 'It's got to be settled before the River Bank party a week before we're supposed to go. Adrian and Letty—'

'I know,' Paul put in, 'they're giving just an intimate little dinner for you and Giles. *Their* Christmas contribution, as it were.'

'I couldn't face it unless all this was resolved,' Rosemary said in a breath. 'Talking about it has been a relief, but made it all the more real.'

'Now we can't bury our heads in the sand any longer,' he agreed, falling back on the cliché.

They looked at each other in mute appeal. Then Paul got up out of his chair, aware that time was hurrying by.

'I've got a consultant to see here,' he exclaimed. Then, putting his hands on her shoulder, he said reassuring, 'I'll be in touch . . . This is not a life for any of us.'

Rosemary's eyes met his with touching confidence. 'I know that whatever you decide will be right.'

He stooped and kissed her cheek.

'I hope to heaven your faith in me will be justified.'

But as he left the flat Paul's mind was a blank. What possible reason could either he or Rosemary give for breaking their respective engagements that wouldn't look contrived or sacrificial?

Tessa bathed and dressed for the party at River Bank, like an automaton. This was the final ordeal. The next time she saw Giles he would be married, and she was by no means sure that he would return to Tewkesbury in any permanent sense. The intervening weeks since his visit to the cottage had passed in numbing emptiness, during which time she had seen him only briefly. His plans had been a subject for general conversation, and she had discussed them with Paul and her parents, trying to switch off her heart from her head.

Now she looked at herself in the long mirror in her bedroom, and saw a stranger. Her black dress of delicate lace, with scalloped neckline, and bodice moulding her breasts, was not in the least sombre, but an elegant understatement of fashion. Womanlike, no matter what the circumstances, she wanted to look her best. Her hair fell loosely about her face and shone in the glow of the carefully arranged lights. All she prayed was that she would be able to get through the evening with sangfroid and live up to the promise she and Giles had made. It helped that Paul had been in London at a medical conference for the past two days, and was returning to go straight to River Bank.

The sustained ringing of the door-bell made her jump and she hurried to answer it; and while she knew with certainty that Giles would never visit her alone again, nevertheless his name filled her thoughts.

A distracted, white-faced patient, Mrs Latimer, whom she knew, stood there.

'It isn't surgery and I should have rung,' she gasped, seeing how Tessa was dressed. 'I'm—' She swayed as she tried to apologise.

Tessa helped her into the sitting room, where she sank into the nearest chair.

'It's quite all right,' Tessa said soothingly, 'just tell me what's wrong.'

'It's my—my son, Jim. He's on drugs—*drugs!*' she repeated in horror. 'You know Jim,' she went on, 'always a reliable boy . . . he's sixteen now. If his father finds out, he'll kill him.' The voice raised to a shriek. 'Oh, Doctor, what can I *do*?'

Tessa said quietly, 'Make quite certain that you're not mistaken. Why do you think he's on drugs?'

'I—I found a syringe and some white powder, and he's been strange—'

'In what way?'

'He's changed . . . his moods, dress, friends. He was such a particular boy; now he doesn't seem to care, and either flies into a temper, or is sullen and morose if you say half a word of criticism.' The woman grew calmer, the drawn lines on her pale face relaxing slightly, a little strength returning to her body as she apologised, 'I'm so sorry to—to have rushed round here like this, and when you're going out, too; but I panicked when I saw the syringe—'

The telephone rang and Adrian asked, 'Everything all right? Only you said—'

'I've got a patient with me at the moment, but I'll be along.' Tessa turned back to Mrs Latimer. 'We've got to be careful not to drive your son deeper into the habit—that is if you're proved to be right. Try to win his confidence without letting him know you suspect.'

'If you could *see* him!'

Tessa was making mental calculations. 'An early diagnosis is important,' she agreed, thinking aloud, 'but the right handling of the case is equally so. Since I *do* call on you from time to time to check up on your bronchitis . . . when is he most likely to be at home?'

'For his tea, about six . . . Oh, and I've missed money once or twice recently . . . told myself I was getting careless.' A despairing little sound escaped Mrs Latimer's lips. 'The stuff has to be bought, after all.'

Tessa's heart sank. The evidence would seem to be indisputable.

'Leave it to me,' she said comfortingly. 'I'll just pop in. Jim and I have often had talks and I can make my own observations. It's useless telling you not to worry,' she added with understanding, 'but keep as calm as you can and make a note of all that goes on.'

'Oh, I will, Doctor, and thank you . . . Jim has always liked you.'

'Getting his confidence is the main thing.'

Mrs Latimer gave a sigh that became a shudder. 'You never think these things will happen in your own family,' she said sorrowfully.

'Can I give you a lift?' asked Tessa.

'Thank you all the same, but I've got to call on a neighbour. Jim's at the sports club.' Mrs Latimer stopped. 'But now I can't trust him to be where he says he is.'

Tessa put out a hand and touched Mrs Latimer's arm. 'Get all the information you can—without appearing to pry,' she counselled again, as she saw her out.

The lighted windows of River Bank shone through the gloom of the misty November evening as Tessa arrived there a little later, and hurried into the hall.

Adrian came towards her.

'Sorry about this,' she murmured, throwing her coat on an ancient settle.

'There's only Giles here,' he said.

Something in his voice arrested her attention. 'Something wrong? It's not like Paul to be late—or Rosemary.'

They went into the drawing room, where Letty and Giles were talking.

'Ah!' exclaimed Letty on a note of relief.

'Hello, Giles.' Tessa's voice was casual and she glanced at him as he got to his feet to greet her. She settled down near Letty, accepting the sherry which Adrian had poured out. 'We didn't wait for you,' Adrian said, indicating their respective drinks. The atmosphere seemed tense, as though they were alerted to some danger. 'I've got a note for you and Giles—from Paul,' he added quietly.

'Note?' Tessa echoed, feeling suddenly faint. She took the envelope, puzzled, enquiring.

'He left it in my care to be given to you this evening,' Adrian added, as he and Letty went from the room.

Tessa looked at Giles half fearfully, the silence filled with suspense as she asked, 'Do you know anything about this?'

'Nothing.' His expression was completely baffled.

'You read it,' she whispered, handing him the envelope.

Giles read aloud,

'Please forgive us for not having the courage to tell you of our feelings and for taking the coward's way out.

When you read this we shall be married.

We shall be back in a week, and hope to make you understand.

Paul and Rosemary'

The address was the Hyde Park Hotel, London.

Tessa gave a little cry of utter disbelief, sitting down weakly on the sofa.

'*Married!*' she gasped, as though doubting the fact.

Giles stared down at the sheet of writing paper in his hand, stunned.

'Paul and Rosemary,' Tessa muttered, her voice shocked with surprise. 'It doesn't seem possible. I mean—' She paused, and hurried on, 'I never for a moment suspected—'

'Nor I,' said Giles adding as he appreciated the absurdity of the statement, 'That was the last hope—too impossible even to think of.'

She stared at him, bewildered, then gasped, 'Oh, Giles, we're free—*free*!' Her voice broke on a note of confused happiness that brought tears to her eyes as he sat down beside her, facing a truth with overwhelming thankfulness, while still fearful to accept it. Emotion reduced them to silence as their hands clasped convulsively.

He said quietly, 'Will you marry me—as soon as possible without giving our secret away?'

'Yes, oh, yes!' she whispered as his arms went around her and his lips met hers.

But they still couldn't quite believe it as they drew apart and continued to look at each other wonderingly, questioningly.

'And to think of all they've gone through before writing that note,' Giles exclaimed, 'even though their circumstances were different. Now I know why Rosemary made an excuse not to see me yesterday . . . she must have gone to London, if not with Paul, then to meet him.' He shook his head. 'I was relieved, and it never occurred to me that—'

Tessa said suddenly, unexpectedly, 'I ought to have guessed.

'How could you possibly have done?' There was doubt in his expression.

'Things she said when she came to see me professionally at the cottage.' Tessa recalled Rosemary's reluctance to go to Singapore, and how she admitted that her earlier readiness to adjust to change was not a true reflection of her desires. The way she had spoken of Paul, as though he possessed qualities she most admired. Tessa could not repeat that confidence, since it was given in a professional context, but she added, 'We're so concerned with our own emotions that we're blind to the conflicts of others, and fit everything neatly into our own pattern.'

Giles looked grave, accepting the truth of the statement.

'Rosemary's state of health . . .' Tessa went on. 'Why should she have been stressed, or strained? It had nothing physically to do with the operation.'

Giles sighed. 'There's irony in the fact that we were so intent upon preserving their happiness that we were blind to their *unhappiness*. Paul has been on edge lately,' he admitted, 'but I told myself I was imagining things because of my own state of mind.'

'I, too,' Tessa confessed, 'whenever Paul was tense or short-tempered—so unlike him.' She gave a little relieved sigh. 'Thank God they had the courage to go, to marry,' she said solemnly. 'For all our sakes.'

'If we'd only known, that night at the cottage,' Giles muttered.

Tessa shook her head. 'Then we shouldn't have that memory, or the satisfaction—'

Their eyes met; she didn't need to finish the sentence. He understood.

The mood changed as Giles said with a smile, 'This will give the gossips a field day!'

'And be a nine days' wonder. Paul is far too popular a figure to lose patients because of a broken engagement and marriage to your fiancée! Our attitude will prevent any drama, and while our continued friendship may give cause for conjecture, it will stabilise the situation. We shall have to be very discreet and allow time to pass before we show any outward interest in each other.'

'Nothing matters,' said Giles, his voice low,' except that one day in the not too far distant future you'll be my wife. We can endure the waiting.'

'You'll have to go to Singapore,' Tessa said quietly.

'Yes; that's as well. The tensions will ease.'

'But you'll continue in the practice?'

'If Paul wishes it—yes.'

Tessa looked troubled. 'Ought we to tell them how we feel? That we love each other?'

'No,' Giles said firmly. 'We couldn't do that without bringing in the reason why *we* didn't break our respective engagements. The circumstances were entirely different, and could cause hurt.' He added, 'Too few words are always better than too many.'

Tessa agreed, then queried, 'Adrian and Letty? What do we tell them? They didn't really believe I was happy in my engagement. I've never been able to keep anything from them yet.'

'We mustn't put them in an invidious position,' Giles said thoughtfully. 'As things stand now, they could only be expected to feel that Paul and Rosemary have let you down.'

'They'll accept my judgment,' Tessa said seriously, 'and I shall ask that there are no hard feelings. I can't play the wronged fiancée—the sheer hypocrisy would sicken me. On the other hand, for us both, discretion and dignity will have to play a part. Adrian and Letty will never ask any questions. And even if I'd been in love with Paul, I hope I'd have generosity of spirit and understanding.' She looked at Giles very earnestly. 'We can sit in their respective chairs—'

'And try to make things as easy as possible for them,' Giles added fervently.

Paul and Rosemary looked at each other across the dinner table.

'They'll know by now,' said Rosemary, and instinctively looked down at the wedding and solitaire diamond rings so newly placed on her finger.

Paul's expression was grave as he said, 'Shall I ever be able to convince myself that this was—was right for you? Not too drastic a step? You deserve so much.'

Her reply was swift and earnest. 'You've given me more peace of mind in these two days than I've known for as many years.' She added unhesitatingly, 'Our marriage was a way out that, even had it occurred to me, I couldn't possibly have suggested.'

'And I don't quite know why it seemed such a simple solution. We don't have to pretend to each other, and we share the same loss,' he added. 'That's an enormous bond.'

They had been married quietly at Marylebone Register Office by special licence that morning, and had made the decision to do so a week previously, Rosemary finding solace as well as relief in the arrangement.

'I don't feel strange with you,' she admitted a little

shyly. 'I never have. I think some instinct must have told us that we were both living in a fool's paradise—if that isn't too harsh a judgment.'

'On the contrary . . . there'll be quite a bit to face in Tewkésbury. Inevitably people will talk, and my being a doctor, to say nothing of the whole medical association, will give the story added interest.'

'We know we haven't let anyone down,' Rosemary said confidently. 'You're far too popular for it to make any real difference . . . Giles and Tessa will be shocked by our note. I wish I could have told Letty; I wouldn't like her to think badly of me.' She paused before adding, half-apologetically, 'I'd hate to lose contact with River Bank, or even to lose Giles' and Tessa's friendship. There's strength in our being together. It will be easier even to *be* with them now, without suspicion and jealousy—all the destructive emotions will lessen because of our relationship. Before, we were fighting alone.'

'How right that is!'

Rosemary fingered her wedding ring.

'I knew, when I talked to Tessa about Singapore that day at the cottage, that I should never marry Giles and that, when she thought about all I'd said, she would so easily make my words fit into the pattern.' She looked around her at the fine dining room with its high ceilings and rich furnishings, feeling a sensation which, while unreal, brought to life a part of her which seemed to have died during the past months—a part that meant freedom from conflict; turbulence, and never-ending fear. She was married, secure, and there was no one except Giles with whom she would rather be than with Paul. She had clung to a vision of life which would never have materialised; a life where the ghost of Tessa would forever haunt her . . . The wound in her heart would take a long while to heal, but it had already ceased to throb, because a decision had been made that was like a merciful bandage.

And, in turn, Paul felt the tension easing as though he had survived some dreaded test. He didn't pretend that the weeks ahead would be easy, but neither would they be fraught with anxiety, indecision, self-criticism, as he refused to face up to the facts that weighed upon him. Tessa had haunted him, her vital arresting charm bewitching him and her gentle acquiescence suddenly filling him with apprehension. The step that he had taken was drastic, but it was also constructive; it would not add wreckage to wreckage; it would prevent both. And in the end would give happiness to two people he loved deeply.

'I hope Giles will stay in the practice,' he said, meeting Rosemary's eyes half-enquiringly.

'Yes . . . we mustn't run away from them; just hope they will understand, and when they eventually marry—'

'It could still be the foursome I'd wanted.' Paul spoke with firmness. 'Thank God you and I haven't any secrets to hide; any fears or heartache we can't share. Things are bound to be difficult,' he added gravely.

'But for the greatest good . . . thank you for making it possible, Paul.'

'It took two,' he reminded her, as he reached out across the table and clasped her hand. 'Now we can be together without pretence.'

'And are already friends,' she murmured with thankfulness. 'The unfairness is that I can't give you children.'

'Not since I don't consider it unfair.' His voice was

strong and sincere. 'We have a marriage to build,' he said confidently. 'That's enough.'

'Yes,' she agreed, consoled, her gaze meeting his in trust and hope.

CHAPTER ELEVEN

THE door closed and Giles and Tessa were alone in their hotel suite at the Tregowen Hotel, near Padstow, having been married quietly earlier that day at Bredon Church.

The June sun fell on the champagne bucket, and the red roses in a nearby vase, as it poured in through balcony windows high up on the cliffs overlooking a secluded beach and the deep blue of the Atlantic. They had not wanted the bustle of airports, and the peace of the converted country house on the Cornish coast was an oasis.

'My *wife*,' Giles said exultantly, drawing her into his arms.

'Oh, Giles,' she whispered, her lips against his, wanting to prolong the excitement that led to the final surrender when the night was theirs and they would sleep in each other's arms.

He sensed her mood and said, 'We've got time to change, although how I'm going to resist you—' He moved to the champagne bucket and lifted the bottle with a flourish. 'We've neither of us drunk or eaten hardly anything today . . . a glass of this, and a few of those canapés, will enable us to survive until dinner!'

'I feel a little drunk already,' she whispered, looking around her at the cream and rose sitting room, with its delicate panelling and deep armchairs. The door leading into the bedroom was open slightly and the furnishings in shades of blue were just visible.

'It's all so beautiful . . .' She went to the wide spacious balcony with its red-and-white awning. 'You could be anywhere in the world,' she added, gazing at the shimmering blue sea on which a thousand sequins seemed to be dancing.

'One of the untouched spots,' said Giles. He moved to her side as she stepped back into the room, and handed her the glass, looking into her eyes as they drank. 'To us, darling,' he said softly.

There was awe in her voice as she murmured, 'I can't think . . . sitting beside you in the car, knowing we were together—'

He stood there, bronzed, powerful, a challenge to her resolution, his fascination making her suddenly a little shy. This man was her husband; there were no barriers, no reservations.

And all the time he was watching her, his gaze holding hers. Memories swirled back: '*We shall meet again; this is not the end.*' He might have been repeating those words as control vanished and she was in his arms, lost to everything but their own need as they moved into the bedroom and sank down on the soft bed. He began to undress her, his hands moving sensuously over her slim body, until her warm smooth limbs curved against him, the touch of his flesh a sudden sharp ecstasy, new, unfamiliar. He looked into her eyes, lost in the passion that surged between them, mounting while he drew her ever closer in that last, quivering rapturous climax. She cried out, her lips seeking his again, all their sexuality finding expression as she whispered his name and heard his stifled, 'I love you, my darling.'

After a short while they lay, arms entwined, desire spent; the warm glow of possession and tenderness remaining as Tessa moved into a comfortable position, her breast against his chest, her head on his shoulder, until they slept.

An hour later, refreshed, looking at each other in disbelief, she whispered, 'Oh, Giles—to be your *wife*!'

He traced the lines of her thighs with his fingers. 'And you had an idea that we could calmly go down to dinner!'

She smiled at him, tantalising, tempting, conscious of his strong, lithe frame turning over so that he leaned on one elbow, gazing down at her, kissing her breast and saying, 'You're so very beautiful . . . how I've resisted you all these months I shall never know.'

Her voice was suddenly quiet, and held a great happiness as she whispered, 'Everything has been worth it to be here like this—free, no shadows . . . seeing Paul and Rosemary happy.' She raised a hand and smoothed his shoulders, feeling a swift stab of emotion and then crying, 'Darling—the *time*!'

Giles' laughter was infectious.

'You won't be taking surgery tonight, Mrs Rutherford; and if I stay here with you another second, you'll be in grave danger of not having any dinner either,' he said, getting out of bed and then lifting her bodily in his arms, his lips on hers as he carried her into the bathroom.

Doctor Nurse Romances

Romance in modern medical life

Read more about the lives and loves of doctors and nurses in the fascinatingly different backgrounds of contemporary medicine. These are the three Doctor Nurse romances to look out for next month.

MIDWIFE MELANIE
Kate Ashton
STOP-GAP DOCTOR
Jennifer Eden
THE PERFECT REMEDY
Frances Crowne

Buy them from your usual paperback stockist, or write to: Mills & Boon Reader Service, P.O. Box 236, Thornton Rd, Croydon, Surrey CR9 3RU, England. Readers in South Africa-write to: Mills & Boon Reader Service of Southern Africa, Private Bag X3010, Randburg, 2125.

Mills & Boon
the rose of romance